Kāla Siddhānta

A complete description of time itself

Karan. N. Londe

Ukiyoto Publishing

All global publishing rights are held by

Ukiyoto Publishing

Published in 2023

Content Copyright © Karan. N. Londe

ISBN 9789360496999

All rights reserved.

No part of this publication may be reproduced, transmitted, or stored in a retrieval system, in any form by any means, electronic, mechanical, photocopying, recording or otherwise, without the prior permission of the publisher.

The moral rights of the author have been asserted.

This book is sold subject to the condition that it shall not by way of trade or otherwise, be lent, resold, hired out or otherwise circulated, without the publisher's prior consent, in any form of binding or cover other than that in which it is published.

DEDICATED TO, AND DICTATED BY
TIME AND DEATH HIMSELF,

ŚIVA

ABOUT THE BOOK

For several hundred years and millennia, Time has always been considered as a part or a reference for any context or subject, however the understanding of the true nature of Time yet remains unaccomplished. This book fulfils and provides a new approach to understanding Time in terms of standardizing all the Time references of different events to a single universal Time unit, enabling us for hypothetical reasoning and answers to the unasked questions like, what is Time? How is it? What's its true nature? What are its effects? Are the effects on us and other things the same? And were all the previous scientists correct about Time? This work also provides complete knowledge of how Time affects an object and explains what actually a Timeline is. This book sets basic understanding of inter dimensional and Multiversal Time travel and communication, which consists of universal Time mechanics, which is applicable for each and every physically bounded structure, right from a single atom to any planetary structure and galaxy. This work will establish a different perception on Time, which will open a new gateway to understanding Time on its basic behavior which will also inherit future technological advancements.

PREFACE

The ancient Indians who were familiar with the concept of Space and Time, were not aware of the theory of relativity. But believed that the duration of time changed from world to world and that our time was not absolute. They distinguished between the cosmic time of the gods and the earthly time of ours. So did the other religions, who had many beliefs. In Hinduism, time is seen as a fundamental aspect of the universe, and is considered to be eternal and unchanging, it also teaches the concept of cyclical time, in which the universe is believed to go through cycles of creation, destruction, and rebirth.

As per the Sacred text, The Bhagavad Gītā, The Supreme Personality of Godhead, Lord Śrī Kṛṣṇa, gives a brief description of time on the battlefield of Kurukshetra to Arjuna.

Lord Śrī Kṛṣṇa says: At the present moment we have just passed through five thousand years of the Kali-yuga, which lasts 432,000 years. Before this there was Dvāpara-yuga (800,000 years), and before that there was Tretā-yuga (1,200,000 years). Thus, some 2,005,000 years ago, Manu (The first being) spoke the Bhagavad-Gītā to his disciple and son.

The age of the current Manu is calculated to last some 305,300,000 years, of which 120,400,000 have passed. Accepting that before the birth of Manu the Gītā was spoken by the Lord to His disciple the Sun-God Vivasvān, a rough estimate is that the Gītā was spoken at least 120,400,000 years ago; and in human society it has been extant for two million years. It was respoken by the Lord again to Arjuna about five thousand years ago. That is the rough estimate of the history of the Gītā, according to the Gītā itself and according to the version of the speaker Lord Śrī Kṛṣṇa.

Further Bhagavata Gītā also gives an insight on the calculation of the duration of time and the conception of multiverse. The duration of universe is limited. It is manifested in cycles of kalpas. A kalpa is a day of Brahmā, and one day of Brahmā consists of a thousand cycles of four yugas, or ages i.e., Satya-yuga, Tretā-yuga, Dvāpara-yuga and Kali-yuga. The cycle of Satya-yuga lasts 1,728,000 years, the Tretā-yuga lasts 1,296,000 years, the Dvāpara-yuga lasts 864,000 years, and finally in Kali-yuga (the yuga we have now been experiencing over the past 5,000 years) lasts 432,000 years. In is said that at the end of the Kali-yuga, Lord Himself appears as the Kalki avatāra, vanquishes the demons, saves His devotees, and commences another Satya-yuga. Then the process is set rolling again. These four yugas, rotating a thousand times, comprise one day of Brahmā, and the same number comprise one night. Brahmā lives one hundred of such "years" and then dies. These "hundred years" by earth calculations total to 311 trillion and 40 billion earth years. By these calculations the life of Brahmā seems fantastic and interminable, but from the viewpoint of eternity it is as brief as a lightning flash. In the Eternal Ocean where Lord Viṣṇu resides, there are innumerable Brahmās rising and disappearing like bubbles. And this is from where the modern concept of multiverse comes from.

Coming back to the world of science, the concept of time has been around as long as humanity has existed, and so does may theories related to it. Many great scientists and their theories have tried to define time, but yet lack to depict the true nature of time in its purest and natural form. It has only been a few centuries where we have come up with many theories and paradoxes related to time. In the ancient Hinduism there also have been many theories and paradoxes, which have been mention in many books, manuscripts, holy texts like Vedas and puranas. But yet they also lack to completely explain the true nature of time. Through ages there has not been a single book on Time so far to our knowledge, it always has been a part of some work, where it has been explained insufficient.

This brought me to a thought, that maybe even the Gods didn't want us to know about the true nature of time or maybe….. we are not yet ready to realize and digest the truth about time.

ACKNOWLEDGEMENT

First of all, this work is dedicated to, and dictated by Shiva himself, The Master of Time. This book would have not been possible without his blessings. I am extremely grateful to Prof. Prasad Hegde, for believing in me and my work. I also would like to thank him for helping me in the course of publishing and for being a guide, a mentor, and an inspiration. I am also grateful to Suryanarayana Bhat, for helping me with Sanskrit.

There have only been a few people to have read and reviewed my book before it was published of which Shrinivas Gavde a colleague from my college, has been a great support and helped me when needed.

Lastly, it would be remiss in not mentioning my family and friends, especially my parents. Their belief in me has kept my spirits high and motivated during this process and supported me during the completion of this book.

Karan Londe

I can destroy the very existence upon which you thrive to survive , with just a mere thought.

You won't even realize until you wake up in another simulated reality , conjured by its desires and lust.

By the time the truth of reality severs your understanding , you are left bewildered realizing me.

I am Kāla, the one who resurrects timelines , the one who holds requiem, the gate to the grave of time.

- Kāla

THIS WORK IS OF PURE DEVOTION

AND HAS BEEN

RESURRECTED BY TIME AND DEATH

HIMSELF

Contents

ADHYĀY – १   1

KĀLA   2
KĀLA VIVARANA   5
STHIRA KĀLA SŪTRA   10
THE LONDE RADIUS   12
ASTHIRA KĀLA SŪTRA   19
KĀLA VYĀPI   28

ADHYĀY – २   51

KĀLA REKHA   52
KĀLA VYĀPI ĀLEKHA   59
MAHAKĀLA   86
KĀLA REKHA ANUNĀDAḤ   90
KĀLA SAṀKRAMAṆAM   95
KĀLA REKHA ŚĀSTRA   101

ADHYĀY – ३   107

PARADOXES AND MYTHS   108

CONCLUSION   110

About the Author   119

ADHYĀY-१

KĀLA

Kāla, Kāla means Time. But Time doesn't mean Kāla, rather Time is one of Kāla's aspect. Where the Time is a part of Kāla. When we say Kāla, what it basically means or referred to as is Time, energy, death, negativity, black, empty, dark, nothing and even sometimes "something". The previously mentioned words are not just synonyms but are a part of that which makes the whole of Kāla. Here in this book, we'll be understanding, experiencing, and referring Time to Kāla.

Primordially, Kāla describes or is referred to Śiva. According to Hinduism, he is one of the Trinity, He is The Auspicious One, The Supreme Being, The Adīyogī, the Mahādevaḥ (God of Gods), The Master of Kāla/Time, The Death himself, The Master of Creation, the very lifeform of existence and also the formless.

Śiva has many names or avatars called as Chandrapal the Master of Moon, Trilochana the Three Eyed, Nagabhushana the Serpent one, Rudra the Fierce Roarer, Nityasundara the ever beautiful, Pushkara the nourisher, Maheshwara the Lord of gods, Ananntadrishti the infinite visionary, Mahayogi the greatest yogi, Vishwanath the master of universe, Jagadisha the ruler of the world and Kāla Bhairava the destroyer of Time.

Śiva is also my Guru, and also the co-author of this book. It is on his will that I have written this book. This book has been directly dictated by Śiva himself, and I have just written this manuscript.

▪ Kāla

Spiritually Kāla or Time is the constant thought flow of Śiva, where his continuous thinking becomes the future, and his previous thoughts are past. Everything works on and according to his own will, the beautiful and peaceful times, where the human race was at its peak of satisfaction. As well as the war, destruction, and plague, where it almost eradicated the great human race. These are his moods, where the peaceful times show his stillness and concentration in his thought, and the destruction represents his anger and discomfort.

Figure 1.1: A Statue of Kāla Bhairava

It is said that when Śiva was in great discomfort, he went on and decided to destroy Time itself. Kāla Bhairava one of the most dangerous manifestation and potent from of shiva. The name itself says Kāla (Time) Bhairava (conquer). Though there are again 8 different manifestations of Kāla Bhairava, the one which went on to destroy Time is not properly depicted in the scriptures.

Why would the creator of Time need any weapons to destroy Time?

KĀLA VIVARANA

Time can be considered in many ways and is often misunderstood as of till now. Time which has no physical form, or anything is something that we are taught from childhood. Time is what we experience. We cannot physically feel Time, yet it is the basis of our existence. Though we don't feel it, it's always around us. To understand Time, first we have to know the Kāla Vivarana i.e., the structure of Time. What is Time? What makes it? How does it behave? What makes Time............TIME? In this part we'll be understanding the structure of Kāla.

- **Kāla Sūtra**

Figure 2.1: Illustration of a Kāla Sūtra

Kāla is made up of Strings/Sutra, called as Kāla Sūtra/Strings of Time. These Sūtra are the basic fundamental unit of Kāla. One can imagine them as a single strand of thread, or a single string from a guitar, unlike these the Kāla Sūtra are non-physical in nature, rather as of now have hypothetical existence. The above Figure 2.1. illustrates a single Kāla Sutra, which is shown with two arrows at each of its ends depicting that Time is eternal and it starts and ends as per one's perspective. As one might see that time is endless, whereas another might not. Therefore, it's not just one or the other Sūtra that make up Kāla, it is made up of innumerable Kāla Sūtra. All perfectly aligned in symmetry just like a manifold. A typical Kāla Sūtra is associated with the properties of Trikālagyana.

▪ Trikālagyana

Trikālagyana means knowledge of all three states of Kāla. One can determine the states of Trikālagyana for a Kāla Sūtra by mere perspective. And these states can be classified into three, which are as follows.

१ Bhūta Kāla (past)

This state of Kāla is considered when according to one's perspective, an object of reference has already experienced a specific targeted event in the Kāla Sūtra.

२ Vartamāna Kāla (present)

This state of Kāla is considered when according to one's perspective, an object of reference is experiencing the specific targeted event in the Kāla Sūtra. "The overlapping of past and future is present".

३ Bhaviśya Kāla (future)

This state of Kāla is considered when according to one's perspective, an object of reference is yet to experience a specific targeted event in the Kāla Sūtra.

This object of reference can be anything, it can be a stone, a device, a planet, an animal or even us. After considering an object of reference, as per our perspective, this object **has**, **is**, or **will** experience the states of Trikālagyana. This experiencing of the states of Trikālagyana, can be considered as a targeted event. Say for example, draw a straight line on a piece of paper, considering it as a Kāla Sūtra. Mark any position on the line and considered it as Vartamāna Kāla or the present, from there to your left side of the line becomes your Bhūta Kāla i.e., past. And from the right of the marked position becomes your Bhaviśya Kāla i.e., future. Therefore, all the incidents that have happened with you, or are happening or are yet to happen can all be considered as a targeted event in the Kāla Sūtra of your own. Further these Kāla Sūtra can be discriminated into two forms.

- **Sthira Kāla Sūtra**

Figure 2.2: Illustration of a Sthira Kāla Sūtra

A Sthira Kāla Sūtra / Constant Strings of Time has no states of Trikālagyana. Due to which Bhūta Kāla, Vartamāna Kāla and Bhaviśya Kāla cannot be experienced as there is no object for reference. Here the dotted circle in the above Figure 2.2. indicates the absence of an object, due to which this type of Kāla Sūtra remains undisturbed or constant.

- **Asthira Kāla Sūtra**

Figure 2.3: Illustration of a Asthira Kāla Sūtra

An Asthira Kāla Sūtra / Disturbed Strings of Time has all the states of Trikālagyana, and all three states can be experienced i.e., Bhūta Kāla, Vartamāna Kāla, and Bhaviśya Kāla. From a point of view, the Vartamāna Kala is experienced, from which we can make out the other two states also, as there is an object for reference. The circle in the above Figure 2.3. indicates the presence of an object, which disturbs the Kāla Sūtra, due to which this type of Kāla Sūtra is Asthira / disturbed.

- **Kāla Gati**

The combination of innumerable Sthira and Asthira Kāla Sūtra which make the whole of Kāla can be visualized as and in Three-Dimensional Euclidian plane, a 3D matrix. (LONDE MANIFOLD), a grid like structure. Stepping into a thought experiment, this three-dimensional Euclidian plane, a 3D matrix can be considered as a hypothetical calm and still ocean, without any waves or current, which represents that Kāla / Time is constant. The only possibility that the ocean can be disturbed is by an object. Where once disturbed, the object tends to flow in a certain direction i.e., towards Bhaviśya Kāla or the future. Which represents that we are flowing through Time towards a specific direction, and not that Time is flowing through or for us.

Therefore, the word Kāla Gati which means velocity or speed of time. Which can be considered as, the drifting of an object through Kāla / Time. Kāla Gati is considered as constant or zero '0', where it doesn't mean it's a null value, instead it determines Kāla is eternal and undisturbed, and that everything starts from zero. The Kāla Gati can be denoted as ' Ξ '.

- ### Kālanubhava

As Kāla Gati is constant, where once we consider an object which is moving through Kāla / Time, some amount of differential time is experienced as it disturbs the constant Kāla / Time and the value of Kāla Gati becomes greater than 0, which signifies that that time is being varied or experienced. This experience of time varies for every other object. therefore, this variable Time experience is called as **Kālanubhava** and can denoted by **Kāla Gati** ' Ξ '.

- ### Precepts for Kālanubhava

१   For any physical object its Kālanubhava can never be zero '0'. And if it is zero '0' then that means the object does not exist physically.

२   The actual Kālanubhava of an object should never be altered.

३   The lower the Kālanubhava the better.

We will be understanding Kāla Gati and Kālanubhava in depth in further chapters.

STHIRA KĀLA SŪTRA

Kāla which is made up of Kāla Sūtra, which defy the laws of physics and mathematics. That's what makes Kāla special. These Kāla Sūtra can be further classified into Sthira and Asthira Kāla Sūtra. Sthira Kāla Sūtra, also called as Undisturbed Strings of Time, are quite easy to understand, as they have no object of reference, which will be explained below.

- **Sthira Kāla Sūtra**

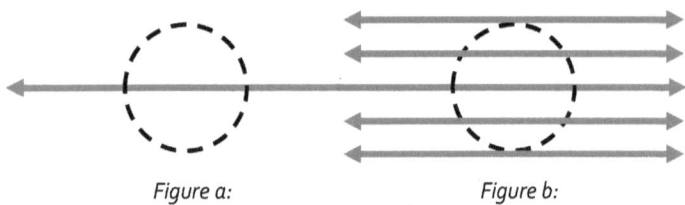

Figure a: *Figure b:*

Figure 3.1: Illustration of a Sthira Kāla Sūtra

Considering the Figure (a), which illustrates a single Sthira Kāla Sūtra, where there is no object of reference, and the Kāla Sūtra is not passing around any object, remains undisturbed. Here the dotted circle represents absence of an object.

Considering the figure (b), which illustrates multiple Sthira Kāla Sūtra and how these Kāla Sūtra are arranged, where there is no object of reference. These multiple Sūtra exhibit a grid like structure which are not passing around any object and remain undisturbed. Here the dotted circle represents absence of an object.

Therefore, we will we not considering this Sthira Kāla Sūtra as they are undisturbed and lack all the states of Trikālagyana, due to absence of an object. Therefore, its Kāla Gati remains '0' or constant.

THE LONDE RADIUS

This part basically deals with the relation between an object and how it disturbs Sthira Kāla Sūtra, resulting in Asthira Kāla Sūtra within a specific boundary called the Londe radius. So, what is this Londe radius?

- **Londe Radius**

The Londe radius is the boundary or the limit within which, Kāla is varied or disturbed and beyond which Kāla is constant. To understand this, we'll jump into a thought experiment and analyses multiple scenarios to understand this concept.

१ **Illustration of Kāla:**

Figure 4.1: Illustration of a Kāla

Considering the above Figure 4.1. as Kāla, where whatever the further incidents or scenarios happen will be taken place within this space. Here the black boundary is the event frame where all the scenarios will take place. Therefore, inside this boundary Kāla is considered as constant, without any disturbances and there is no object disturbing it. Here we will be considering the future scenarios to be in 2-Dimension only for ease of our understanding.

२ **Illustration of an object in Kāla:**

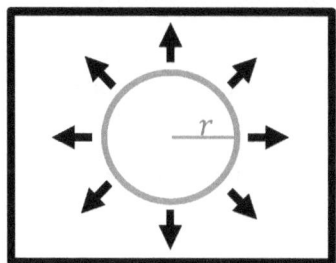

Figure 4.2: Illustration of an object in Kāla

When an object with radius 'r' arises in Kāla, there will be disturbance in Kāla. Where this object will occupy a certain area in Kāla. Due to which it will push the same amount of area which it is occupying outwards as shown in the above Figure 4.2.

Now, considering the first circle: $A_r = \pi r^2$ .... (1)

3 **Illustration of Pushed out Kāla by object:**

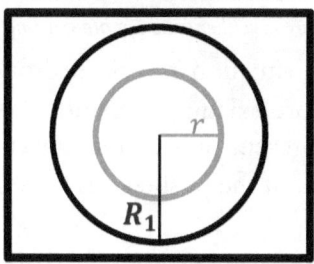

Figure 4.3: Illustration of pushed out Kāla by an

14 Kāla Siddhānta

As seen in the previous scenario, an object occupying a specific area in Kāla, pushes the Kāla that was previously occupying the area outwards. This pushed out Kāla will form another circle of radius 'R_1' outside the object as shown in the above Figure 4.3.

Now, considering the second circle:

$$A_{R1} = \pi R_1^2 \quad \text{... (2)}$$

the whole area of circle 'R_1' can also be considered as,

$$A_{R1} = 2A_r \quad \text{.. (3)}$$

This pushed-out Kāla can be considered as Disturbed Kāla.

౮ **Illustration of pre-existing Kāla:**

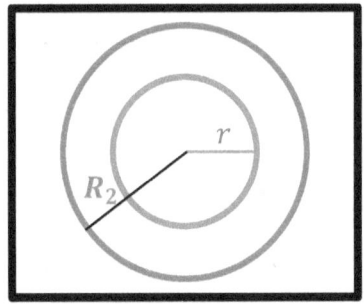

Figure 4.4: Illustration of pre-existing Kāla

Here in this situation the pushed-out Kāla 'R_1' will overlap the pre-existing undisturbed Kāla 'R_2' which is naturally present outside the object which will have the same area of the pushed out Kāla 'R_1', as shown in the Figure 4.4.

Now, considering the third circle:

$$A_{R2} = \pi R_2^2 \quad \text{...............................} \quad (4)$$

We also get, $A_{R2} = 2A_r$ .... (5)

ງ   Illustration of overlapping of Kāla:

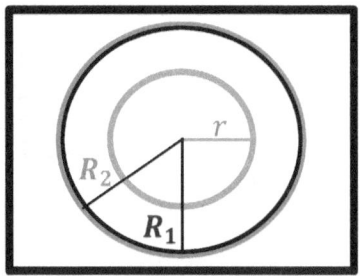

Figure 4.5: Illustration of overlapping of Kāla.

In this case the undisturbed Kāla 'R_2' will be overlapped by or stacked upon by the disturbed Kāla 'R_1', as shown in the above Figure 4.5. Which will later be condensed to form a new circle 'K_R' as shown in the next Figure 4.6.

Therefore, Overlapping will be,

$$A_{K_r} = A_{R1} + A_{R2} \quad \text{..............................} \quad (6)$$

Here A_{K_r} will have area of A_{R1} and A_{R2}, but with the same radius. Which can be written as,

$$R_1 = R_2 = K_R \text{...} (7)$$

Here the overlapping will give rise to a 3-Dimensional

situation but will be considered in 2-Dimensional only.

६   Illustration The Londe radius:

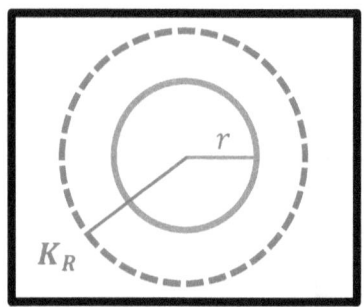

Figure 4.6: Illustration of The Londe radius

From equation (6),
$$A_{K_r} = \boldsymbol{A_{R1}} + A_{R2} \quad \text{... (6)}$$
$$A_{K_r} = \boldsymbol{A_{R1}} - A_r + A_{R2} - A_r \quad \text{......................... (8)}$$
$$A_{K_r} = \boldsymbol{A_{R1}} + A_{R2} - 2A_r \quad \text{............................. (9)}$$
Substituting (3) and (5) in (9),
$$A_{K_r} = 2A_r + 2A_r - 2A_r \quad \text{............................. (10)}$$
$$A_{K_r} = 2A_r \quad \text{... (11)}$$
Now to find K_R ,
$$A_{K_r} = 2A_r \quad \text{... (11)}$$
$$\pi K_R{}^2 = 2\pi r^2 \quad \text{... (12)}$$
$$K_R = r\sqrt{2} \quad \text{... (13)}$$

Therefore, **The Londe radius** $(K_R = r\sqrt{2})$,is mathematically derived. Hence, the Londe radius is the limit or the boundary beyond which Kāla becomes constant and within which Kāla is varied or experienced.

The Figure 4.7. illustrates an object bounded by the Asthira Kāla Sūtra, till a certain limit or a boundary called the Londe radius and beyond this boundary Kāla becomes constant i.e., Sthira Kāla Sūtra.

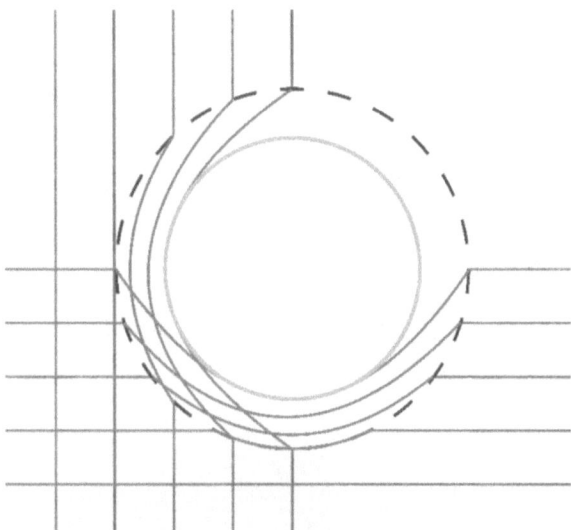

Figure 4.7: Illustration of an object with its Londe radius and disturbance in Kāla

This Londe radius can be applied to any object which has an area with a positive radius. If an object has an irregular shape or a shape rather than a circle, we need to approximate it and considered it as a circle. This Londe radius can be applied to anything right from an atom to planets and galaxies to living things such as us, humans to animals and etc.

For example, if we consider a circle of radius 10 cm. Then, its Londe radius $'K_R'$ will be,

$K_R = r\sqrt{2}$
$K_R = 10\sqrt{2}$
$K_R = 14.14243562$

ASTHIRA KĀLA SŪTRA

As we already know the Sthira Kāla Sūtra and its characteristics, we now proceed to the next part of this understanding, The Asthira Kāla Sūtra. In this part we'll understand how Time exists and comes into existence.

- **Asthira Kāla Sūtra**

As previously explained an Asthira Kāla Sūtra has all the states of Trikālagyana, and all the three states are experienced, due to the presence of an object for reference. Further to calculate this experiencing of time, we follow the following steps.

- **Asthira Kāla Sūtra equation for Londe radius**

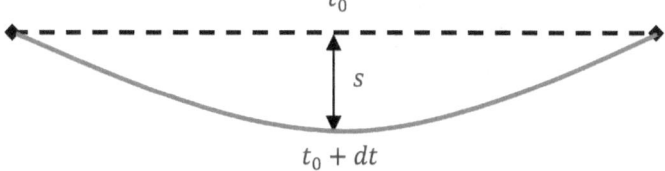

Figure 5.1: Illustration of Asthira Kāla Sūtra equation for Londe radius

This Asthira Kāla Sūtra equation for Londe radius calculates the difference between Sthira and Asthira Kāla Sūtra, As shown in the Figure 5.1. Where the dotted line can be considered as a Sthira Kāla Sūtra and the curve as Asthira Kāla Sūtra.

$$t_0 + dt = t_0 + \frac{S}{\sqrt{2}}$$

Here,

$t_0 + dt$ = Asthira Kāla Sūtra.
t_0 = Sthira Kāla Sūtra.
S = Sag.

- **Asthira Kāla Sūtra Predictor Formula**

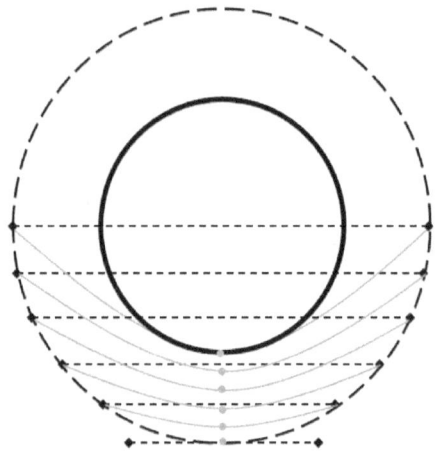

Figure 5.2: Illustration of an object with its Londe radius and Asthira Kāla Sūtra

The above Figure 5.2. depicts the arrangement of Sthira Kāla Sūtra which represent the dotted lines and the Asthira Kāla Sūtra which represent the curve to its respective dotted line from the center of the figure to the bottom of it. To predict the position of Asthira Kāla Sūtra around an object within its Londe radius, this formula divides the objects radius as well as its Londe radius by no. of divisions required.

To predict the positions of Sthira Kāla Sūtra inside the whole of the Londe radius, where the black dotted lines represent Sthira Kāla Sutra as shown in the Figure 5.2. is given by,

$$\frac{K_R}{n}$$

To predict the positions of Asthira Kāla Sūtra around the object and within the Londe radius, where the curves represent Asthira Kāla Sūtra as shown in the Figure 5.2. is given by,

$$\frac{(K_R - r)}{n}$$

Therefore, we can represent it like this,

$$\frac{(K_R - r)}{n} \equiv \frac{K_R}{n}$$

- ### Kāla Vyāpi Bindu.

An object with its Londe radius, has multiple **Kāla Vyāpi Bindu** i.e., Points of Variance, for each of its Asthira Kāla Sūtra with its own Kāla Gati and these points represent different levels of Kālanubhava. To calculate these Kāla Vyāpi Bindu, we need to equate in the following steps.

१ Object selection:

Identification of an object is necessary, in order to calculate its Time variance. The conditions for selection of an object are:

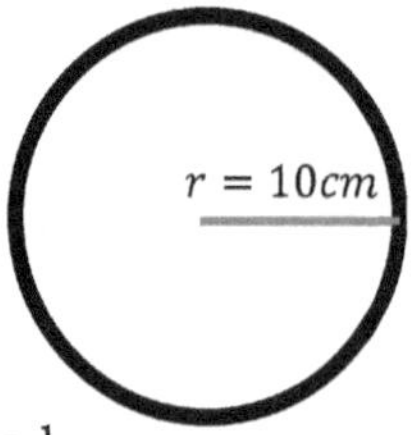

a) For ease of calculation only spherical or a circle are considered as an object.

b) Though the object may be in irregular shapes, which can be rather than a circle. We will approximate it and assume it into a circle.

c) The selected object must have area with a positive radius.

Figure 5.3.

Here, for example we are considering a 2-Dimensional object i.e., a circle of radius 10m as shown in the Figure 5.3.

२ Calculation of the Londe Radius:

Once an object is selected we, then need to find the Londe radius of that object .i.e.

The Londe radius of an object with 10 m of radius will be,

$K_R = r\sqrt{2}$

$K_R = 10\sqrt{2}$

$K_R = 14.14213$

$K_R \approx 14$

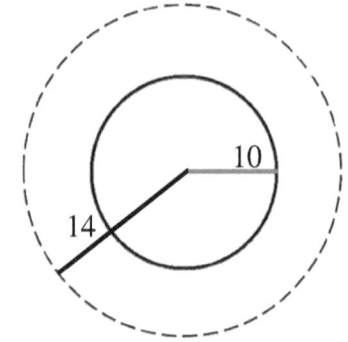

Figure 5.4: Illustration of the Londe radius for a 10m circle

Therefore, the Londe radius of the object is
$K_R \approx 14\ cm$.

3   Applying the Asthira Kāla Sūtra Predictor Formula:

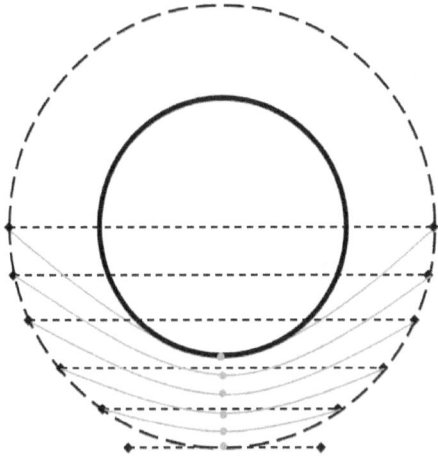

Figure 5.5: Illustration of an object with its Londe radius and Asthira Kāla Sūtra

Now we must use the Asthira Kāla Sūtra Predictor formula to calculate the number of Asthira Kāla Sūtra around the object.

Here, let be 'n' the no. of divisions to be = 5, and substitute the necessary values.

Then,

$$\frac{(K_R - r)}{n} \equiv \frac{K_R}{n}$$

$$\frac{(14-10)}{5} \equiv \frac{14}{5}$$

$$0.8 \equiv 2.8$$

Here the above result means, 5 division of 2.8 m each for the 14 m radius circle i.e., the Londe radius.

And 5 division of 0.8 m each for the 10 m radius circle i.e., the selected object.

4. Finding Kāla Vyāpi Bindu using the Asthira Kāla Sūtra equation:

After applying the Asthira Kāla Sūtra predictor formula, we further name each Asthira Kāla Sūtra accordingly i.e., $t_0, t_1, t_2, t_3, t_4, t_5$ and then calculate its Kāla Vyāpi Bindu by applying the Asthira Kāla Sūtra equation. (The further calculations are shown below).

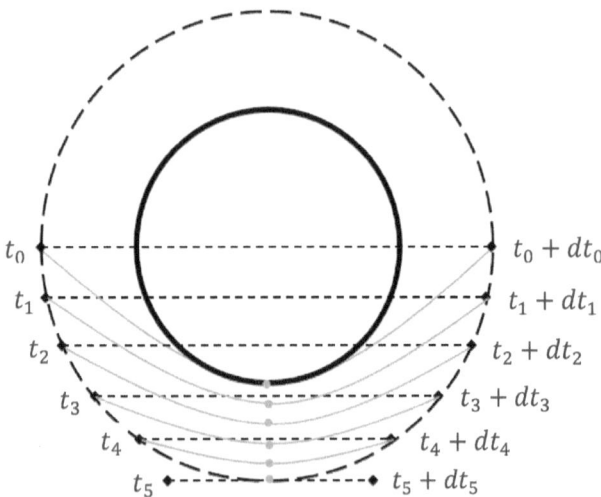

Figure 5.6: Illustration of an object with its Sthira and Asthira Kāla Sūtra

For Sūtra t_0,

$$t_0 + dt_0 = t_0 + \frac{S}{\sqrt{2}}$$

$$t_0 + dt_0 = 28 + \frac{10}{\sqrt{2}}$$

$$t_0 + dt_0 = 35.07106 \approx 36$$

$$dt_0 = 8 \ \Xi$$

For Sūtra t_1,

$$t_1 + dt_1 = t_1 + \frac{S}{\sqrt{2}}$$

$$t_1 + dt_1 = 27.5 + \frac{8}{\sqrt{2}}$$

$$t_1 + dt_1 = 33.15685 \approx 33$$

$$dt_1 = 5.5 \ \Xi$$

For Sūtra t_2,

$$t_2 + dt_2 = t_2 + \frac{S}{\sqrt{2}}$$

$$t_2 + dt_2 = 25.5 + \frac{6}{\sqrt{2}}$$

$$t_2 + dt_2 = 29.74264 \approx 29.5$$

$$dt_2 = 4 \ \Xi$$

For Sūtra t_3,

$$t_3 + dt_3 = t_3 + \frac{S}{\sqrt{2}}$$

$$t_3 + dt_3 = 22 + \frac{4}{\sqrt{2}}$$

$$t_3 + dt_3 = 25.3284 \approx 24.5$$

$$dt_3 = 2 \ \Xi$$

For Sūtra t_4,

$$t_4 + dt_4 = t_4 + \frac{S}{\sqrt{2}}$$

$$t_4 + dt_4 = 17 + \frac{2}{\sqrt{2}}$$

$$t_4 + dt_4 = 18.41421 \approx 18$$

$$dt_4 = 1 \ \Xi$$

For Sūtra t_5,

$$t_5 + dt_5 = t_0 + \frac{S}{\sqrt{2}}$$

$$t_5 + dt_5 = 0 + \frac{0}{\sqrt{2}}$$

$$t_5 + dt_5 = 0$$

$$dt_0 = 0 \ \Xi$$

5. Plotting the Kāla Vyāpi Bindu:

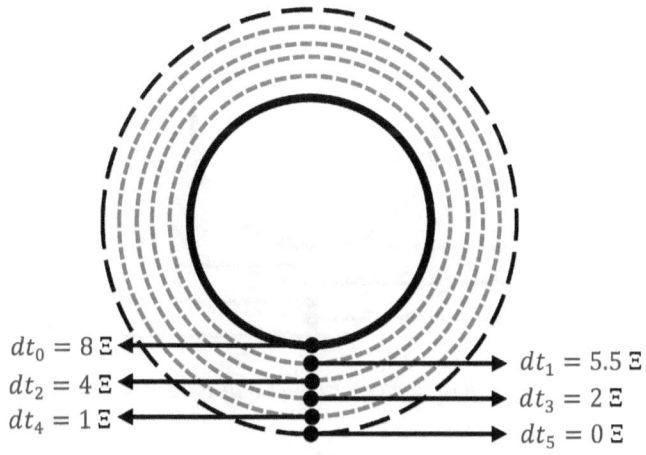

Figure 5.7: Illustration of an object with its Kāla Vyāpi Bindu

These points are **Kāla Vyāpi Bindu**, which are unique to every object and exhibit **Kāla Vyāpi** / Time Variance at a specific point only. These points are the differences of Kāla Gati of each of the following Asthira Kāla Sutra considered. At these Kāla Vyāpi Bindu, Kālanubhava can be experienced. Here a gradience is observed where the highest value is on the surface of the object and gradients to zero '0' as it nears the boundary of its Londe radius. Therefore, the Kāla Vyāpi Bindu on the surface on any objects is considered as important and used in most of the calculations. This Kāla Vyāpi Bindi can be considered as Kālanubhava at a specific point on an object.

6. Kāla Vyāpi Paridhi:

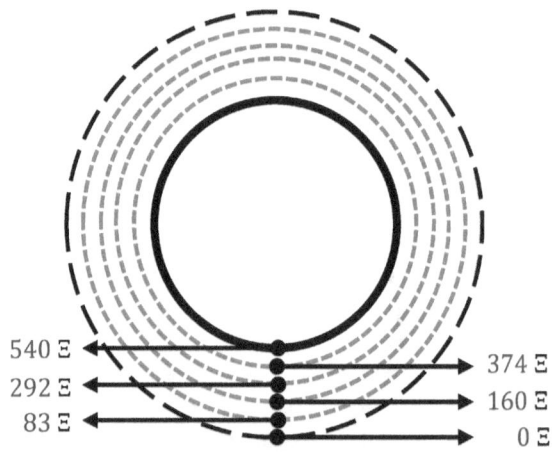

Figure 5.7: Illustration of an object with its Kāla Vyāpi Bindu

The Kāla Vyāpi Bindu only exhibits Kāla Vyāpi at a specific point only, whereas when we multiple these Kāla Vyāpi Bindu to the circumference where these Kāla Vyāpi Bindu are positioned, it will give us Kāla Vyāpi Paridhi. This Kāla Vyāpi Paridhi can be considered as the total Kālanubhava of an object. We only consider on surface Kāla Vyāpi Paridhi. Which means that for this object of radius 10 m, its total time experience will be 540 Ξ.

KĀLA VYĀPI

In this part we will be know the true importance of the Kālanubhava and Kāla Vyāpi Bindu, by applying all that we have learnt so far in this book to multiple example and see different case scenarios. Also, we will be standardizing all the time units and references to a single unit.

- ### Kāla Vyāpi

Kāla Vyāpi / Time Variance is the differential Kālanubhava / Time experience at different levels of Kāla Vyāpi with respect to its Kāla Vyāpi Bindu, which are represented in terms of Kāla Gati.

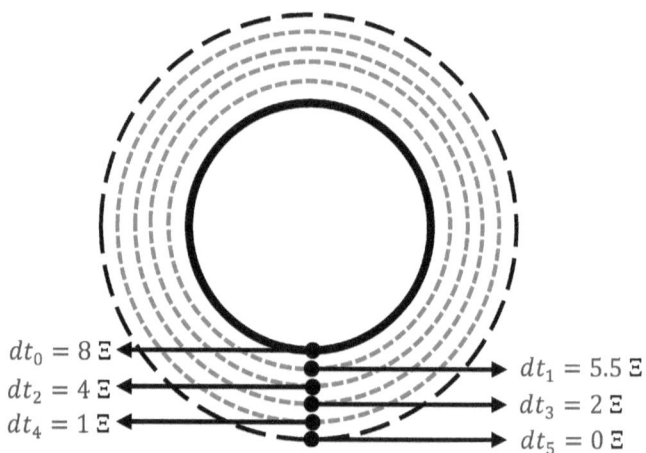

Figure 5.7: Illustration of an object with its Kāla Vyāpi Bindu

As shown in the above Figure 6.1, each Kāla Vyāpi Bindu has its own respective circle i.e., Kāla Vyāpi Paridhi, which indicate levels of Kāla Vyāpi, where these levels determine the Kāla Gati. Each level varies, where the level dt_0 on the surface of the object has the highest Kāla Vyāpi and the level dt_5 that is the outermost level, which is the boundary of the Londe radius has the lowest or the least Kāla Vyāpi, and beyond which Kāla becomes constant i.e., 0 as per the Kala Gati.

Considering level dt_0, dt_3 and dt_5, where each have different Kāla Vyāpi Bindu and will also have different Kāla Vyāpi. At level dt_0 the Kāla Vyāpi will have a greater Kāla Gati and Kālanubhava compared to the other two levels i.e., dt_3 and dt_5. At the level dt_5 the value of Kāla Vyāpi Bindu is zero '0' Kāla Gati, therefore the Kāla Gati will be constant as consider in its original state. By using the Kāla Vyāpi Bindu, we can make out the Kāla Vyāpi, and represent it in terms of Kala Gati. Therefore, by using the previous procedure we can calculate the Kāla Vyāpi details of any object.

- **Kāla Kṣetra Proportionality**

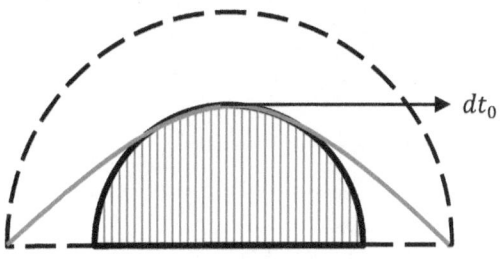

Figure 6.2.

This equation gives the relation between area and Kāla. Here the Kṣetra / Area of an object is directly proportional to its Kāla Vyāpi Bindu. As the area of an object increases, there is also an increase in its Kāla Vyāpi Bindu which is represent in Kāla Gati.

$Area \propto Kāla$

$Kṣetra \propto Kāla\,Vyāpi\,Bindu$

$Kṣetra = K \times Kāla\,Vyāpi\,Bindu$

$Kṣetra = 4.44 \times r \times Kāla\,Vyāpi\,Bindu$..........

$(K = 4.44 \times r)$

- **General Cases of Kāla Vyāpi**
१ **Single object's Kāla Vyāpi**

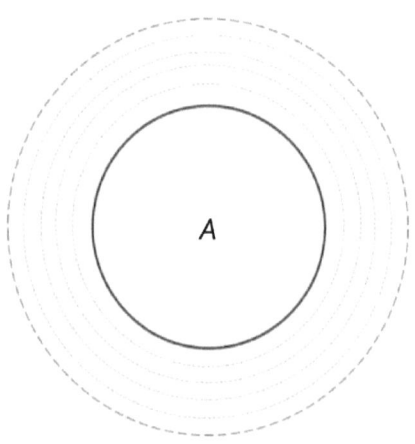

Figure 6.3.

Details of the given object A.

radius (r) = 10.0 m
Londe radius (K_r) = 14.142135623730951
Sthira Kāla Sūtra (t_0) = 28.284271247461902
Asthira Kāla Sūtra $(t_0 + dt_0)$ = 35.35533905932738
Kāla Vyāpi Bindu (dt_0) = 7.0710678118654755 Ξ
Kāla Vyāpi Paridhi = 444.2882938158366 Ξ

For the given object of radius 10 m, the above is the Kāla Vyāpi details. As already explained in the previous chapter the Kāla Vyāpi details for the given object, which implies the same here.

२ **Two objects Time Variance**
a. **Case 1:**

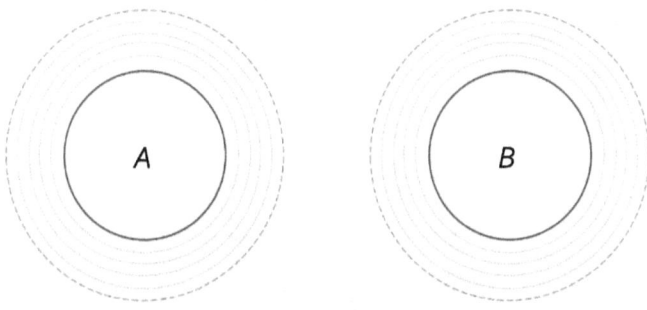

Figure 6.4.

Details of the object A.

radius $(r) = 10.0$
Londe radius $(K_r) = 14.14213562373$
Sthira Kāla Sūtra $(t_0) = 28.2842712474$
Asthira Kāla Sūtra $(t_0 + dt_0) = 35.35533$
Kāla Vyāpi Bindu $(dt_0) = 7.071067811\ \Xi$
Kāla Vyāpi Paridhi $= 444.28829381583\ \Xi$

Details of the object B are as same as object A.

For the given case, considering 2 objects with same radius which are separated by a specific distance, which won't affect their respective Kāla Vyāpi. Therefore, both the objects will have their respective individual Kāla Vyāpi and will not affect each other. Above are the Kāla Vyāpi details of both the objects.

b.　　Case 2:

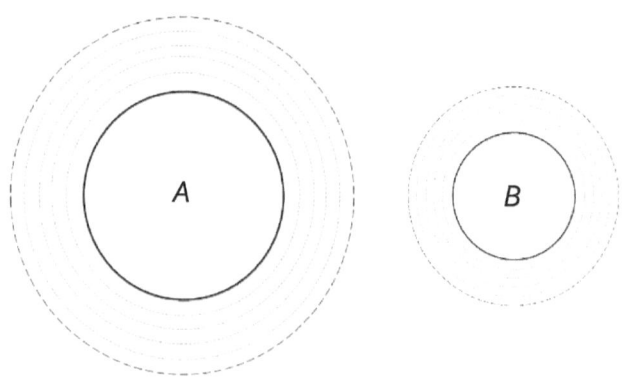

Figure 6.5.

Details of the object A.

radius $(r) = 10.0$
Londe radius $(K_r) = 14.14213562373$
Sthira Kāla Sūtra $(t_0) = 28.2842712474$
Asthira Kāla Sūtra $(t_0 + dt_0) = 35.35533$
Kāla Vyāpi Bindu $(dt_0) = 7.071067811\ \Xi$
Kāla Vyāpi Paridhi $= 444.28829381583\ \Xi$

Details of the object B.

radius $(r) = 6.0$
Londe radius $(K_r) = 8.485281374238$
Sthira Kāla Sūtra $(t_0) = 16.9705627484$
Asthira Kāla Sūtra $(t_0 + dt_0) = 21.2132$
Kāla Vyāpi Bindu $(dt_0) = 4.24264068\ \Xi$
Kāla Vyāpi Paridhi $= 159.9437857737\ \Xi$

For the given case, considering 2 objects with different radius which are separated by a specific distance, which won't affect their respective Kāla Vyāpi. Therefore, both the objects will have their respective individual Kāla Vyāpi and will not affect each other. Above are the Kāla Vyāpi details of both the objects.

c. **Case 3:**

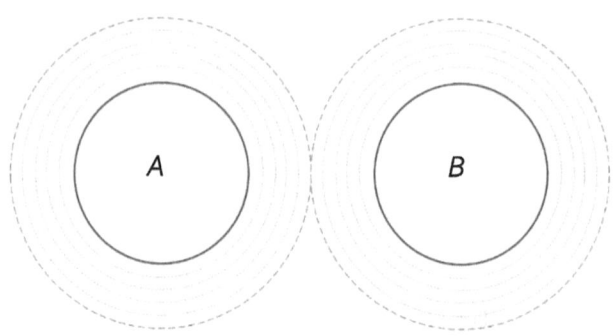

Figure 6.6.

Details of the object A.

radius (r) = 10.0
Londe radius (K_r) = 14.14213562373
Sthira Kāla Sūtra (t_0) = 28.2842712474
Asthira Kāla Sūtra $(t_0 + dt_0)$ = 35.35533
Kāla Vyāpi Bindu (dt_0) = 7.071067811 Ξ
Kāla Vyāpi Paridhi = 444.28829381583 Ξ

Details of the object B are as same as object A.

For the given case, considering 2 objects of same radius, of which their boundary of Londe radius is touching each other, which won't affect their respective Kāla Vyāpi, as the Kāla Vyāpi Bindu and Kāla Vyāpi Paridhi on the londe radius boundary will be 'zero'. Therefore, both the objects will have their respective individual Kāla Vyāpi and will not affect each other. Above are the Kāla Vyāpi details of both the objects.

d. Case 4:

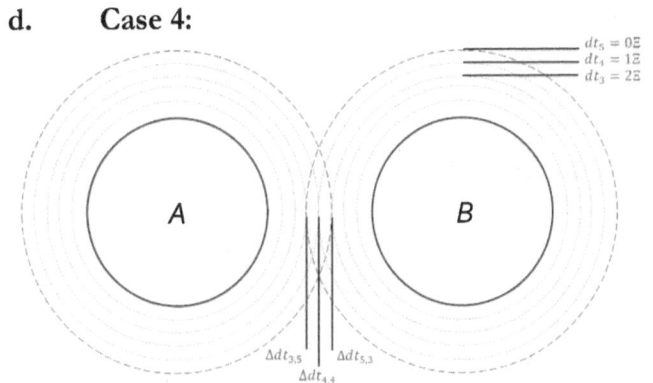

Figure 6.7.

Details of the object A.

radius (r) = 10.0
Londe radius (K_r) = 14.14213562373
Sthira Kāla Sūtra (t_0) = 28.2842712474
Asthira Kāla Sūtra $(t_0 + dt_0)$ = 35.35533
Kāla Vyāpi Bindu (dt_0) = 7.071067811 Ξ
Kāla Vyāpi Paridhi = 444.28829381583 Ξ

Details of the object B are as same as object A.

For the given case, considering 2 objects of same radius, of which their Londe radius is being shared. Here dt_5, dt_4 and dt_3 are the levels of Kāla Vyāpi that are being shared by both the objects, where $dt_5 = 0$ Ξ, $dt_4 = 1$ Ξ and $dt_3 = 2$ Ξ are the Kāla Vyāpi Bindu.

The first level of Kāla Vyāpi That is being shared is dt_3 of object A and dt_5 of object B which results in,

$$\Delta dt_{3,5} = dt_3 + dt_5 = 2\ \Xi$$

The second level of Kāla Vyāpi That is being shared is dt_4 of object A and dt_4 of object B which results in,
$$\Delta \boldsymbol{dt_{4,4}} = dt_4 + dt_4 = 2\,\Xi$$

The third level of Kāla Vyāpi That is being shared is dt_5 of object A and dt_3 of object B which results in,
$$\Delta \boldsymbol{dt_{5,3}} = dt_5 + dt_3 = 2\,\Xi$$

Hence an increase is observed in the Kāla Gati at dt_5, dt_4 and dt_3, which will also affect Kālanubhava at those Kāla Vyāpi levels.

e. **Case 5:**

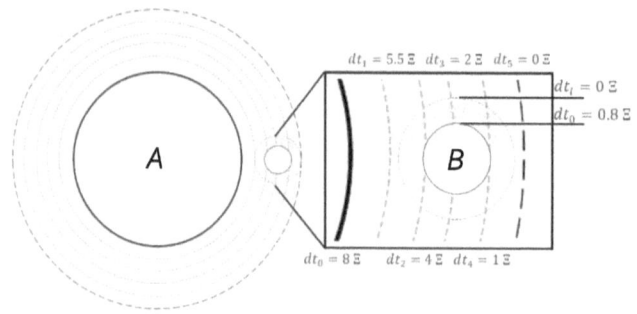

Figure 6.8.

Details of the object A.

radius $(r) = 10.0$
Londe radius $(K_r) = 14.14213562373$
Sthira Kāla Sūtra $(t_0) = 28.2842712474$
Asthira Kāla Sūtra $(t_0 + dt_0) = 35.35533$

Kāla Vyāpi Bindu (dt_0) = 7.071067811 Ξ
Kāla Vyāpi Paridhi = 444.28829381583 Ξ

Details of the object B.
radius (r) = 1.2
Londe radius (K_r) = 1.6970562748477
Sthira Kāla Sūtra (t_0) = 3.394112549695
Asthira Kāla Sūtra $(t_0 + dt_0)$ = 4.242640
Kāla Vyāpi Bindu (dt_0) = 0.848528137 Ξ
Kāla Vyāpi Paridhi = 6.3977514309480 Ξ

For the given case, considering 2 objects A & B of different radius, where object B is positioned inside the Londe radius of the object A between dt_2 and dt_4, and the whole of object B along with its Londe radius is situated between dt_1 and dt_5 as shown in the Figure 6.8.

Above are the Kāla Vyāpi details of object A and B, through which we can calculate the difference in Kālanubhava for the object B which is Situated inside the Londe radius of object A. When a smaller object is situated inside a larger object's Londe radius, the smaller object will be dominated by the larger object. Here the domination means the total change in its Kāla Gati and Kālanubhava and its Kāla Vyāpi details for the smaller object. This domination only affects the small object which are around larger objects.

Therefore, the Domination of object A on B and change in its Kāla Gati and Kālanubhava for object B can be calculated accordingly.

The first level of Kāla Vyāpi That is being shared is dt_1 of object A and dt_l of object B which results in,
$$\Delta dt_{1,l} = dt_1 + dt_l = 5.5 \; \Xi$$

The second level of Kāla Vyāpi That is being shared is dt_2 of object A and dt_0 of object B which results in,
$$\Delta dt_{2,0} = dt_2 + dt_0 = 4.8 \; \Xi$$

The third level of Kāla Vyāpi That is being shared is dt_4 of object A and dt_2 of object B which results in,
$$\Delta dt_{4,0} = dt_4 + dt_2 = 1.8 \; \Xi$$

The fourth level of Kāla Vyāpi That is being shared is dt_5 of object A and dt_l of object B which results in,
$$\Delta dt_{5,l} = dt_5 + dt_l = 0 \; \Xi$$

By the above results, the object B's side facing towards object A will have a greater Kāla Gati and Kālanubhava compared to the other side of object B. Overall, the Kāla Gati increases compared to its actual Kāla Vyāpi details of object B. Therefore, we can say that Kāla Vyāpi and Kālanubhava of object B increases when it is dominated by Object A. whereas, the Kāla Vyāpi of object A remains the same.

f.   **Case 6:**

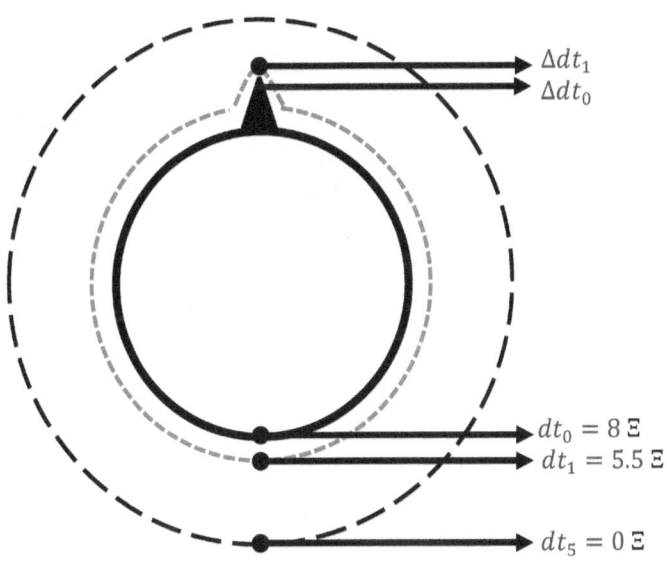

Figure 6.9.

Details of the object A.

radius $(r) = 10.0$
Londe radius $(K_r) = 14.14213562373$
Sthira Kāla Sūtra $(t_0) = 28.2842712474$
Asthira Kāla Sūtra $(t_0 + dt_0) = 35.35533$
Kāla Vyāpi Bindu $(dt_0) = 7.071067811$ Ξ
Kāla Vyāpi Paridhi $= 444.28829381583$ Ξ

For the given case, considering an object of radius 10m, with all its Kāla Vyāpi details given above. Here this circle has an expansion in the shape of a triangle as shown in the above Figure 6.9, which for example can be considered as a mountain. As we already know that this circle will bend the Kāla Sūtra and Kāla Vyāpi is experienced, therefore this expansion will also bend the Kāla Sūtra a little more near the expansion area. This expansion will have an increase in its value of Kāla Vyāpi Bindu, on and around the expansion region compared to the value of Kāla Vyāpi Bindu on the surface of the circle, as shown in the Figure 6.9. This change in value is represented as, Δdt_n. Here for our understating, we are only considering dt_0 and dt_1 Kāla Vyāpi Bindu, where due to the presence of expansion region the change we get is, $\Delta dt_0 > dt_0$ and $\Delta dt_1 > dt_1$. Here dt_5 does not go under any change.

- **Live examples of Kāla Vyāpi**

Now that we have been through multiple cases and scenarios which explained and depicted how the Kāla Sūtra behave. Let's, now apply these case studies on live examples to observe and experience Kālanubhava and standardize all time units and references.

१ The Human Body

Till now we all might have wonder that, can we predict the life expectancy of our body using this concept? And the answer is no, we cannot predict the life expectancy of a human body. The human body is made up cells, tissues, organs, and organ systems, which is a complex and is a highly organized structure that works together to perform certain function to sustain something that what we call as 'life'. This is a biological form that decays by time and has an average life span of 70 years. Though many scientists suggest, and a few came up with theories, saying that we might live a lot more years in space than on earth and also if we travel at the speed of light we might never really get old. Therefore, this makes a total of 70 earth years, as an average life span for a human being. I remember a quote from Karl Marx, he says "Time was invented by clock companies to sell more clocks". Here on earth, we have multiple units to represent time, like seconds, minutes, hours, days, months, years, and now even Light years for space travel. But these all units are related to earth as we consider it as reference. As scientists consider Mathematics as the single language of the universe, lets also consider a single unit of time by standardizing all time units and reference to a single unit.

Figure 6.10: Illustration of a human body by Leonardo Da Vinci

An average adult Human is around 5.6 feet (170 cm) and weighs around 70 kgs. Therefore, to calculate its Kāla Vyāpi details we need to first calculate its Londe radius by consider this human body as a sphere. When we approximate it into a sphere its radius will be around 20 centimetres.

Therefore, the Kāla Vyāpi details of the human body will be,
radius (r) = 20 cm
Londe radius (K_r) = 28.284271247461902
Kāla Vyāpi Bindu (dt_0) = 14.142135623730951 Ξ
Kāla Vyāpi Paridhi = 1777.1531752633464 Ξ

Here the Kāla Vyāpi Paridhi means that, the whole of human body has a total Kāla Gati of 1777.15 Ξ, which also means that the human body is flowing through Kāla / Time at a Kāla Gati of 1777.15 Ξ, this can be considered as the total time experience or the Kālanubhava of the human body. Here we are not considering any other parameters. Therefore, a Human experiences / has a Kālanubhava of 1777.15 Ξ.

२ Earth
Just like Sir. Carl Sagan said, "Look again at that dot. That's here. That's home. That's us." Here we'll be considering our planet Earth and apply all the concepts that we have learnt so far.

Figure 6.11: Picture of the pale blue dot

Kāla Vyāpi details of the Earth.

radius (r) = 6371.0 km
Londe radius (K_r) = 9009.95460587899
Sthira Kāla Sūtra (t_0) = 18019.90921175798
Asthira Kāla Sūtra $(t_0 + dt_0)$ = 22524.88651469747
Kāla Vyāpi Bindu (dt_0) = 4504.977302939493 Ξ
Kāla Vyāpi Paridhi = 180335023.46487322 Ξ

Here the Kāla Vyāpi Paridhi means that, the whole of planet Earth has a total Kāla Gati of 180335023.464 Ξ, which also means that Earth is flowing through Kāla / Time at a Kāla Gati of 180335023.464 Ξ, this can be considered as the total time experience or the Kālanubhava of Earth. Here we are not considering any other parameters such as gravity, etc. Therefore, Earth experiences / has a Kālanubhava of 180335023.464 Ξ.

Here the Kāla Vyāpi Bindu (dt_0) means that, at any point on the surface of Earth the Kāla Gati will be 4504.977 Ξ, which also means that on any point on the surface of Earth, if an object exists then it is flowing through Kāla / Time at a Kāla Gati of 4504.977 Ξ, where that object's Kāla Vyāpi Paridhi is also added up. This can be considered as the time experience or the Kālanubhava at any point on the surface of Earth for an object.

Now coming to the question, what would be the Kālanubhava of a human on earth. To calculate this the Kāla Vyāpi Paridhi of a human will be added with the Kāla Vyāpi Bindu (dt_0) of Earth as we consider the human to be on the surface. Therefore, the Kālanubhava of the Human being on Earth will be,

Kāla Vyāpi Paridhi of human + Kāla Vyāpi Bindu of Earth

1777.153 Ξ + 4504.977 Ξ = 6282.127 Ξ

Hence, the Kālanubhava of the Human being on Earth will be 6282.127 Ξ, where we observer an increase in its Kāla Gati on Earth compared to its actual Kāla Gati, i.e., its Kāla Vyāpi Paridhi which is 1777.153 Ξ.

Coming back to the **precepts for Kālanubhava**. Where the second precept says, the actual Kālanubhava of an object should never be altered. Which means that, the actual Kālanubhava i.e., its Kāla Vyāpi Paridhi of a human is altered on earth, where we observe an increase in its Kālanubhava. Therefore, this precept of Kālanubhava is being violated.

The third precept says, the lower the Kālanubhava the better. Where this precept is associated to an object's lifespan. As the Kālanubhava increase the lifespan decrease, and as the Kālanubhava decrease the lifespan increases for an object (living or non-living). Therefore, as we humans residing on earth is not beneficial to our Kālanubhava, where a human can live longer in outer space than on earth.

3 **Mars**

Figure 6.12: Picture of planet Mars

Kāla Vyāpi details of the Mars.

radius (r) = 3390.0 km
Londe radius (K_r) = 4794.183976444792
Sthira Kāla Sūtra (t_0) = 9588.367952889585
Asthira Kāla Sūtra $(t_0 + dt_0)$ = 11985.459941111982
Kāla Vyāpi Bindu (dt_0) = 2397.091988222397 Ξ
Kāla Vyāpi Paridhi = 51058055.013609774 Ξ

Here the Kāla Vyāpi Paridhi means that, the whole of planet Mars has a total Kāla Gati of 51058055.013609774 Ξ, which also means that Mars is flowing through Kāla / Time at a Kāla Gati of 51058055.013609774 Ξ, this can be considered as the total time experience or the Kālanubhava of Mars. Here we are not considering any other parameters such as gravity, etc. Therefore, Mars experiences / has a Kālanubhava of 51058055.013609774 Ξ.

Here the Kāla Vyāpi Bindu (dt_0) means that, at any point on the surface of Mars the Kāla Gati will be 2397.091 Ξ, which also means that on any point on the surface of Mars, if an object exists then it is flowing through time/Kāla at a Kāla Gati of 2397.091 Ξ, where that object's Kāla Vyāpi Paridhi is also added up. This can be considered as the time experience or the Kālanubhava at any point on the surface of Mars for an object.

Let's now consider us, a human on the surface of Mars. Therefore, the Kālanubhava of the Human being on Mars will be,

Kāla Vyāpi Paridhi of human + Kāla Vyāpi Bindu of Mars

1777.153 Ξ + 2397.091 Ξ = 4174.241 Ξ

A decrease total 2107.886 Ξ is observed in the Kālanubhava of the human on Mars compared to Earth. Therefore, as per the third precept of Kālanubhava, A human can live longer on Mars compared to Earth.

- **Special Cases of Kāla Vyāpi**
- १ **Speed of light**

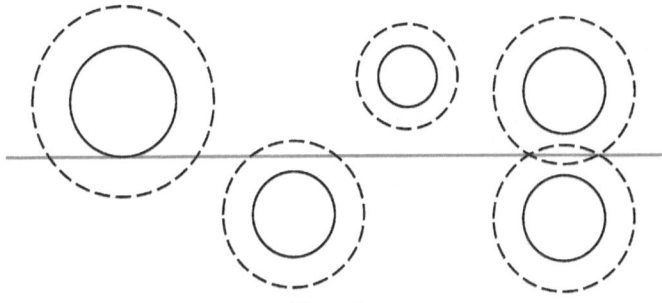

Figure 6.13:

Considered the above Figure 6.13, which has many objects of different sizes with their respective Kāla Vyāpi cases and can be considered as planets. The figure also has a line which passing through few of the planets. Say a human is traveling along this line from left to right of the figure, where he passes through these planets with their Kāla Vyāpi cases and will experience a change in his Kālanubhava. The human will experience a change in his Kālanubhava as long as he remains inside the Londe radius of the respective planet. When inside the Londe radius, of a large object the Kālanubhava of the human will be greater compared to objects small in size.

Here the velocity of the human traveling through the objects can be equal to or less than the **speed of light**, as it doesn't matter, because as long as the human is under the dominance of any object his Kālanubhava will vary.

२ BLACK HOLE

A Black hole consists of ergosphere and photonsphere as the outer most region, followed by the event horizon and the singularity at the center. Here the event horizon is determined by the Schwarzschild's radius, but the singularity is a point which has zero radius and infinite density, which is caused when a core collapses completely into itself. It is said that time ceases to exist as we near the event horizon and even the light cannot escape the black holes gravity.

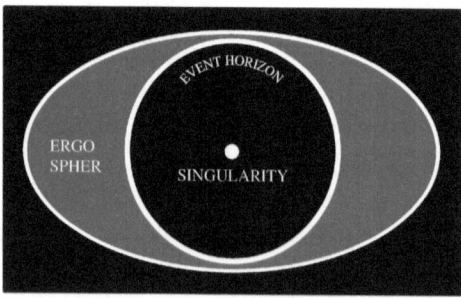

Figure 6.14: Illustration of a Black hole

According to Kāla Vyāpi we can come up with two cases.

Case 1 (zero physical radius): The physical part of a black hole is its singularity which has zero radius and has high density. Where according to the first precept of Kālanubhava this object does not exist physically, and when it does not exist there won't be any Kāla Vyāpi and Kālanubhava, resulting to kāla Gati being zero '0'. Therefore, any object inside the event horizon will only purely experience its actual Kālanubhava and will not be under any dominance. This can show that time slows down as we near a black hole, compared to physically larger radius object.

Case 2 (negative radius): There can also be a possibility where the singularity can have a negative radius, where this doesn't make any sense. If considered a negative radius then the Londe radius of the object will also become negative and the Kāla Vyāpi Bindu will also have negative values resulting in negative Kāla Vyāpi, where we already know that time cannot be in negative terms.

3 Dominance of universe, galaxies, and planetary systems

Figure 6.15: Picture of a Galaxy

As we have already seen the dominance of larger objects on smaller objects, the same goes with this concept of understanding. In our ball shaped observable universe which compromising of all the matter that can be observed, also holds several hundred billion galaxies. Where a galaxy is a system of stars, planetary systems, stellar remnants, interstellar gas, dust, dark matter etc., which are bounded by time and gravity. A star may dominate or get dominated by a larger star, which will be dominated by another and so on, depicts the planetary system. the planetary system is also dominated or dominate several other planetary systems forming the shape of a galaxy. These galaxies are also dominate and are dominate by several other galaxies in our universe. Therefore, if we calculate this dominance to its peak then, we can observe a huge change in our Kālanubhava.

ADHYĀY-२

KĀLA REKHA

As soon as we know we are there, it's not even there. Kāla Rekha / Timeline one of the biggest misconception of the modern and ancient sciences, where people often misunderstood timelines and multiverse to be the same. Here we will understand the complete knowledge of Kāla Rekha, its behaviors, types, properties, effects, causes and most importantly, Rules that are supposed to be followed.

- **Kāla Rekha**

The natural displacement of an object in Kāla from Bhūta Kāla to Bhaviśya Kāla, where the object is bounded by the Kāla Sūtra is called an Kāla Rekha / Timeline. Here the object flows through Kāla.

- **Types of Kāla Rekha**

१ Asthira Kāla Rekha

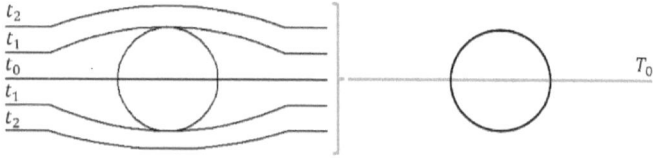

Figure 7.1: Illustration of an Asthira Kāla Sūtra to an Asthira Kāla Rekha

This Kāla Rekha is made up of Asthira Kāla Sūtra i.e., which are disturbed by an object. As shown in the Figure 7.1, $'t_n'$ number of Sūtra is considered as a whole of a single Asthira Kāla Rekha. These Kāla Rekha can be represented as a single line through a body of reference as shown in the Figure 7.1. Asthira Kāla Rekha is represented by T_n (ex: T_0). This is the Kāla Rekha in which we all and everything exist.

र Sthira Kāla Rekha

Figure 7.2: Illustration of a Sthira Kāla Sūtra to a Sthira Kāla Rekha

This Kāla Rekha is made up of Sthira Kāla Sūtra. Since there is no object of reference, there won't be any Kāla Rekha of any importance and hence it can be neglected. This type of Kāla Rekha is also represented as T_n (ex: T_0). This is the Kāla Rekha in which nothing exists.

▪ Types of Asthira Kāla Rekha

This Asthira Kāla Rekha is unique and has a certain characteristic, which allows it to develop multiple choices and is capable of choosing only one choice on its own will, where this choice predict its future. This Asthira Kāla Rekha lies in a state of superposition, until a choice is made. Further this Asthira Kāla Rekha can be discriminate into two types based on superposition of its choices.

१ Single Stem Asthira Kāla Rekha

This is the basic Asthira Kāla Rekha. Here, this single Asthira Kāla Rekha is capable of developing only one choice, i.e., to continue to remain as a single Asthira Kāla Rekha.

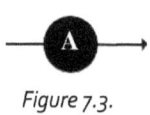

Figure 7.3.

Considering a thought experiment, where the circle 'A' will have only one choice and will continue to remain in its same state as shown in the Figure 7.3.

२ Branched Asthira Kāla Rekha

This is a complex Asthira Kāla Rekha, where it capable of developing 'n' number of choices, which further results into branching of 'n' number of Single Stem Asthira Kāla Rekha. For example, if the number of choices is limited to 3.

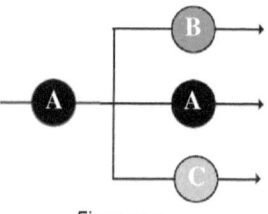

Figure 7.4.

Then this Asthira Kāla Rekha continues to be in a state of superposition until a single choice is made and its superposition breaks down to one single reality. Considering a thought experiment, where the circle 'A' will have three choices to change to i.e., ('A', 'B', and 'C'). Further after making a choice, it can remain in its state or continue branching as shown in the Figure 7.4.

Types of Branched Asthira Kāla Rekha

These further branching of Asthira Kāla Rekha can be classified into two types based on the occurrence of its choices.

१ Symmetric Branching

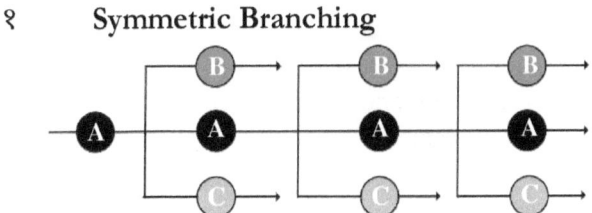

Figure 7.5.

Here the branches are symmetric, where choices are repeated with symmetry for a Asthira Kāla Rekha as shown in the Figure 7.5. Here there can be 'n' number of choices which will keep on repeating for the 'N' number of times in the same Asthira Kāla Rekha. Considering a thought experiment where, the number of choices is limited to 3, and a circle 'A' will have symmetric branches, where symmetric choices will keep on appearing i.e., ('A', 'B', and 'C'). Further after making a choice, it can remain in its state or again continue branching as shown in the Figure 7.5.

२ Asymmetric Branching

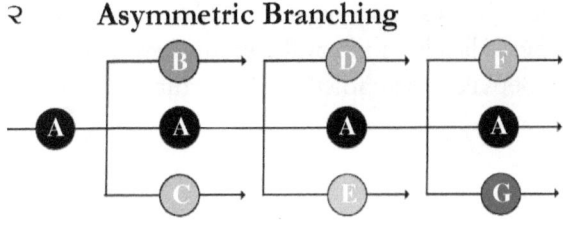

Figure 7.6.

Here the branches are asymmetric, where choices repeat without any symmetry for a Asthira Kāla Rekha as shown in the Figure 7.6. Here 'n' number of choices will keep on repeating for the 'N' number of times in the same Asthira Kāla Rekha. Considering a thought experiment where, the number of choices is limited to 3, and a circle 'A' will have asymmetric branches, where asymmetric choices will keep on appearing i.e., ('A', 'B', 'C', 'D', 'E', 'F', 'G' and so on). Further after making a choice, it can remain in its state or again continue branching as shown in the Figure 7.6.

▪ Types of Intervals in Branched Asthira Kāla Rekha

These Symmetric and Asymmetric Branching of Asthira Kala Rekha can be further classified based on the occurrence of choices in the Kāla Rekha.

१ Regular branching intervals

Here the choices are predictable, which happen periodically in regular intervals. Here the choices are branchings. There are equal intervals between the choices or branching in the Kāla Rekha.

२ Irregular branching intervals

Here the choices are unpredictable, which don't happen periodically in intervals. Here there is unequal intervals between the choices or branching in the Kāla Rekha.

- ## Kāla Rekha Nāmakaraṇa / Naming of the Timelines

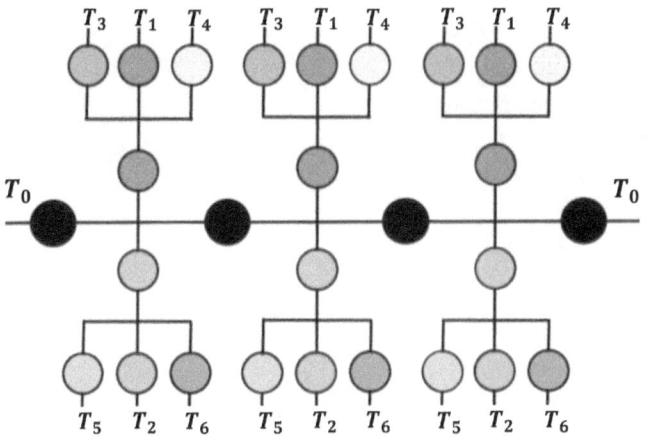

Figure 7.7: Illustration of a Branched Kāla Rekha

T_0 is the Mūlā Kāla Rekha, or the main Kāla Rekha and its point of origin is called as the Mūlādhāra. Further this Kāla Rekha can branch into multiple other Sub Kāla Rekha such as T_1, T_2, T_3 etc. Here each Kāla Rekha is unique, and are further needed to predict the desired outcome, to achieve this we need to identify and name each possible Kāla Rekha. By using this notation, we can name multiple Kāla Rekha and predict the outcomes possibility.

$n_b T_n \langle n_{sb} sT_n |$

Here,

T_n : Kāla Rekha.
n_b : branch number.
sT_n : Sub Kāla Rekha.
n_{sb} : Subbranch number.

For example,
$1 T_0 \langle 2 T_1 \langle 1 T_4 |$

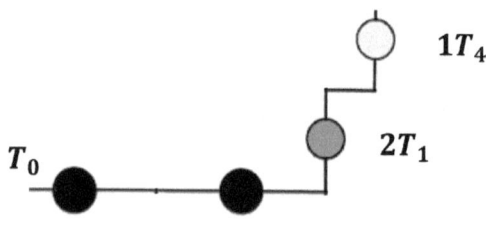

Figure 7.8.

KĀLA VYĀPI ĀLEKHA

Timelines, a very delicate word. When mentioned, another word associated with it arrives in our mind, "Time travel". When heard of it, many fantasies, movies, hypothesis are well versed, where for over the centuries this word has been misunderstood. Here in this part, we'll be understanding the complete behavior of the Kāla Rekha / Timeline, as it is, by looking at a very delicate part of it in a very sophisticated way. This mind-bending concept of Time is where we plot the Kāla Rekha into a simple yet very sophisticated understandable graphs. These Kāla Rekha are the predictions of how we flow through Kāla, and how the proper flow of Kāla can be maintained. These Kāla Vyāpi Ālekha / Time Variant Graphs are plotted, understood, and only exits in the Londe Manifold.

- **The Londe Manifold**

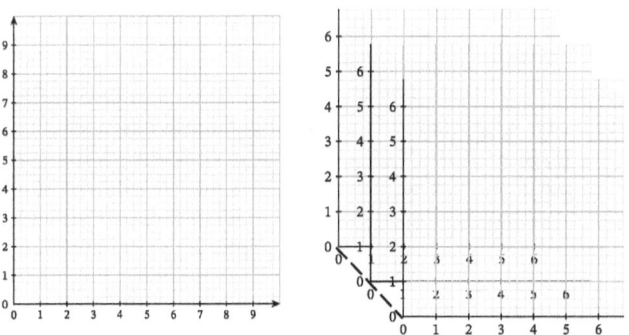

Figure 8.1: Illustration of the Londe Manifold

This is unlike any other manifold that we have known. This manifold is like Euclidian manifold, where only the first quadrant is considered. Just as the first quadrant of the Euclidean plane, this manifold also consists of 2 axis which set a boundary for the Kāla Rekha, where both the axis are equivalent and are represented in positive values, as Time can never be negative. (x = y for cartesian form & $dt_0 = dt_0$ for Londe Manifold). Though considering Two axis representing the same into 2 dimensions, understanding this becomes complicated when we try to represent it into a 3-dimensional manifold. Here the 2-dimensional manifolds are placed or stacked upon one another, which makes it to be considered as a 3-dimensional manifold.

- **Kāla Rekha Prayana**

Kāla Rekha Prayana $(\varkappa)$ is the unit used to denote the displacement of a Kāla Rekha in Kāla. Here $'\varkappa'$ represents positive values on both the axis of the Londe Manifold which determines the displacement of a Kāla Rekha. This is a scalable unit and can use any time reference like seconds, minutes, years, light years and so on. From now on, this manifold will be the basis of everything that we are going to understand about Kāla Rekha, and plot accordingly.

- ## Kāla Vyāpi Ālekha

Kāla Vyāpi Ālekha / Time Variant Graph can also be represented using Einstein's metric tensor. The graph that we will be seeing in the future of this theory are only represented in the Londe manifold. Here the two axis of Londe manifold which make up a quadrant define a limit for the graph beyond which a Kāla Rekha should not exceed or cross, if else the behavior of the Kāla Rekha changes, this limit or boundary of the quadrant is called the **Kāla Vyāpi Sīmā**. **Mūlādhāra** the root of existence of the Kāla Rekha or can be considered as a starting point of a Kāla Rekha. When plotted, a linear graph is obtained, this linearity can be considered as a mathematical representation of **Kāla Rekha**. The primordial Kāla Rekha that arises from the Mūlādhāra is called as **MūlāKāla Rekha.** This unconditional linearity is also called as **Predicated Kāla Rekha Trajectory**. This linearity predicts the trajectory of a Kāla Rekha, which is an important behavior to maintain the proper flow of Time. Any Kāla Rekha that satisfies the above **Kāla Vyāpi Ālekha Conditions** will maintain the proper flow of Time and is called as **Kāla Vyāpi Rekha/Time Variant Timeline**. Considering a Kāla Rekha T_0 where it keeps on extending i.e., $t_0 + dt$ as shown in the Figure 8.2. Using the metric tensor, we plot the Kāla Vyāpi Ālekha on the londe manifold as follows.

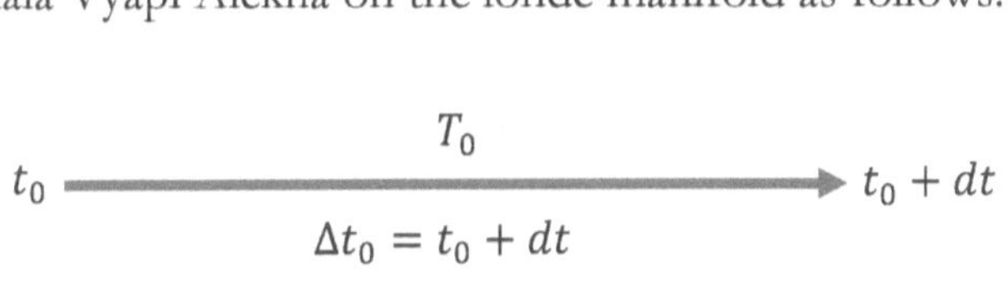

$$t_0 \xrightarrow{\quad T_0 \quad} t_0 + dt$$
$$\Delta t_0 = t_0 + dt$$

Figure 8.2.

$(\Delta t_0)^2 = (t_0 + dt - t_0)^2$
$(\Delta t_0)^2 = (dt)^2$ ....($x_2 - x_1$)
$(\Delta t_0)^2 = (dt_0)^2$ ....($dt \to dt_0$)

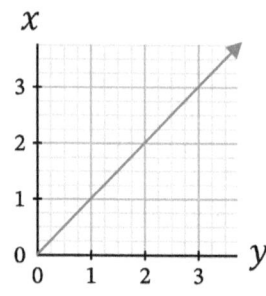
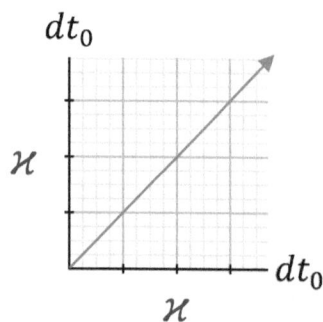

For Cartesian form:
$(\Delta t_0)^2 = 1(dt)^2$
$(\Delta t_0)^2 = 1.\, dt_0.\, dt_0$
$(\Delta t_0)^2 = 1 dt_0.\, 1 dt_0$
$(\Delta t_0)^2 = 1x.\, 1y$ ....($dt_0 \to x, y$)

For Londe Manifold:
$(\Delta t_0)^2 = \varkappa (dt_0)^2$
$(\Delta t_0)^2 = \varkappa.\, dt_0.\, dt_0$
$(\Delta t_0)^2 = \varkappa dt_0.\, \varkappa dt_0$

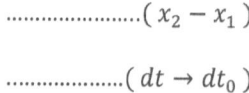

This linearity can as be represented as
$x = y$ …………...for Cartesian form
$dt_0 = dt_0$ …………..for Londe Manifold

These are the general equations of the Kāla Rekha and their respective Kāla Vyāpi Ālekha. Here dt_0 represent both the axis as shown in the graph, where '$ϰ$' is a scaling factor and determines Kāla Rekha Prayana. $ϰdt . ϰdt$ means that value '$ϰ$' lies on both the axis and is being varied.

▪ Three Behavioral States of Kāla Vyāpi Ālekha.

१ Sthira Kāla Vyāpi Ālekha

A Sthira Kāla Vyāpi Ālekha / Stable Time Variant Graph is considered as stable in nature if it satisfies all the above Kāla Vyāpi Ālekha Conditions. This is how almost all Kāla Rekha are and should behave, which maintains the proper flow of Kāla. This is the most basic Kāla Rekha and will be consider in upcoming topics.

For Londe Manifold:
$(\Delta t_0)^2 = ϰ(dt_0)^2$
$(\Delta t_0)^2 = ϰ . dt_0 . dt_0$
$(\Delta t_0)^2 = ϰdt_0 . ϰdt_0$
$(\Delta t_0)^2 = ϰdt_n . ϰdt_n$

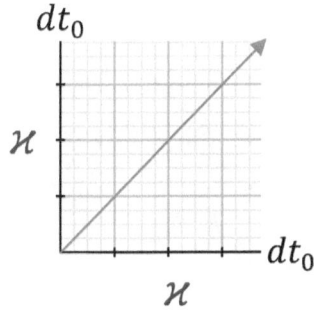

$x = y$ …………...for cartesian form
$dt_n = dt_n$ …………...for Londe Manifold

These are 2 most rare and uncertain cases.

२ Asthira Kāla Vyāpi Ālekha

This is considered as an Asthira Kāla Vyāpi Ālekha / Unstable Time Variant Graph because it does not satisfy the Kāla Vyāpi Ālekha Conditions, due to its offset in Predicted Kāla Rekha Trajectory, its Kāla Rekha doesn't maintain its linearity, which results instability of the Kāla Rekha. This Asthira Kāla Rekha manages to be within the limits of the Kāla Vyāpi Sīmā, which eventually may cross through and give rise to the forbidden state of the Kāla Rekha. This is that type of Kāla Rekha which should not be maintained.

For Londe Manifold:
$(\Delta t_0)^2 = \varkappa (dt_0)^2$
$(\Delta t_0)^2 = \varkappa . dt_0 . dt_0$
$(\Delta t_0)^2 = \varkappa dt_0 . \varkappa dt_0$

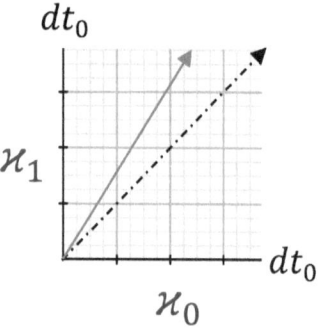

$(\Delta t_0)^2 = \varkappa_0 dt_0 . \varkappa_1 dt_0$ …………...$(\varkappa \to \varkappa_0, \varkappa_1)$

$(\Delta t_0)^2 = \varkappa_0 dt_n . \varkappa_1 dt_n$

$x = n\, y$ …………...for cartesian form
$dt_n = N\, dt_n$ …………...for Londe Manifold

3   Niṣiddha Kāla Vyāpi Ālekha

Niṣiddha Kāla Vyāpi Ālekha / Forbidden Time Variant Graph is a total catastrophe. When an Asthira Kāla Vyāpi Ālekha's Kāla Rekha keeps on continuing to be in that state, which has a complete offset from its trajectory and crosses the Kāla Vyāpi Sīmā, this happens. This is not supposed to happen as it may lead to loops in Kāla / Time which will definitely lead to many Time paradoxes. We will understand this in depth in upcoming concepts.

For Londe Manifold:
$(\Delta t_0)^2 = \varkappa (dt_0)^2$
$(\Delta t_0)^2 = \varkappa . dt_0 . dt_0$
$(\Delta t_0)^2 = \varkappa dt_0 . \varkappa dt_0$

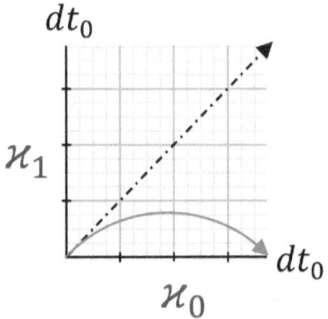

$(\Delta t_0)^2 = \varkappa_0 dt_0 . \varkappa_1 dt_0 \quad \ldots\ldots\ldots (\varkappa \to \varkappa_0, \varkappa_1)$

$(\Delta t_0)^2 = \varkappa_0 dt_n . \varkappa_1 dt_n$

$\sum (\Delta t_0)^2 = \varkappa_0 dt_n^i . \varkappa_1 dt_n^i$

$$\sum_{i=1}^{m} (\Delta t_0)^2 = \varkappa_0 dt_n^i . \varkappa_1 dt_n^i$$

- ### Kāla Vyāpi Khaṇḍa

A Kāla Rekha has multiple points across its predicted trajectory called as **origin points**. The first origin point of any Kāla Rekha is called as the **Mūlādhāra**. Each of these points across the Predicted Kāla Rekha Trajectory can be used as a reference to make out a Kāla Vyāpi Ālekha. Each defined origin point will have its own Kāla Vyāpi Ālekha. Multiple Kāla Vyāpi Ālekha with respect to its origin points on a single Kāla Rekha can be called as **Kāla Vyāpi Khaṇḍa / Time Variant Frames**. Any origin point across a Kāla Rekha can be considered as an Mūlādhāra. But, if we keep on changing the Mūlādhāra to the different origin points then the past information of the Kāla Rekha is lost. As the Mūlādhāra is considered as the starting point or source of any Kāla Rekha. Here, Number of origin points on a Kāla Rekha is equal to the Number of Kāla Vyāpi Khaṇḍa / Time Variant frames on a Kāla Rekha.

८   Kāla Vyāpi Khaṇḍa of a Single Stem Sthira Kāla Vyāpi Ālekha

Considering the Figure 8.3. where a Kāla Rekha T_0 for the Kāla Vyāpi Ālekha dt_0, has three origin points of which one is the Mūlādhāra with their respective Kāla Vyāpi Ālekha i.e., dt_0^1, dt_0^2, dt_0^3 which are the Kāla Vyāpi Khaṇḍa. The Kāla Rekha T_0, can be calculated by diving the main Kāla Vyāpi Ālekha into three Kāla Vyāpi Khaṇḍa, which can be calculated separately as shown in the below figures.

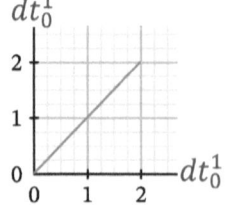

Kāla Vyāpi Khaṇḍa dt_0^1,

$(\Delta t_0^1)^2 = \varkappa dt_0^1 \cdot \varkappa dt_0^1$
$(\Delta t_0^1)^2 = 2dt_0^1 \cdot 2dt_0^1$

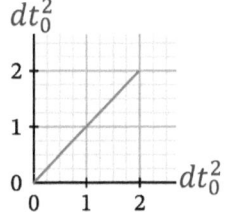

Kāla Vyāpi Khaṇḍa dt_0^2,

$(\Delta t_0^2)^2 = \varkappa dt_0^2 . \varkappa dt_0^2$
$(\Delta t_0^2)^2 = 2dt_0^2 . 2dt_0^2$

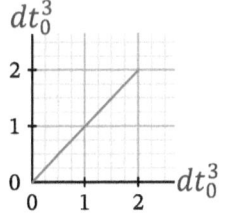

Kāla Vyāpi Khaṇḍa dt_0^3,

$(\Delta t_0^3)^2 = \varkappa dt_0^3 . \varkappa dt_0^3$
$(\Delta t_0^3)^2 = 2dt_0^3 . 2dt_0^3$

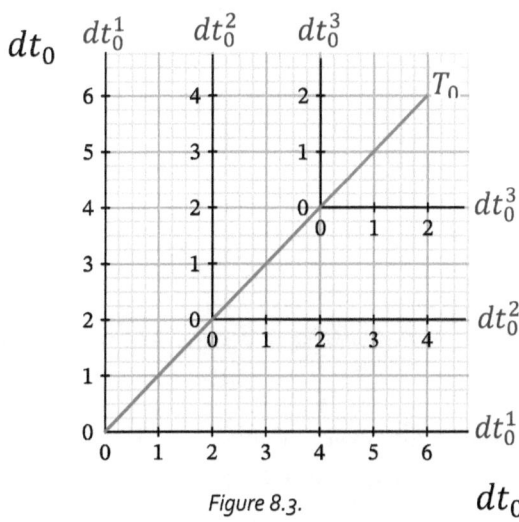

Figure 8.3.

Kāla Vyāpi Khaṇḍa dt_0,

$(\Delta t_0)^2 = n\, dt_0 . n\, dt_0$
$(\Delta t_0)^2 = 6 dt_0 . 6 dt_0$

Therefore, we can say that Kāla Vyāpi Ālekha dt_0 is equal to the sum of all other Kāla Vyāpi Khaṇḍa. i.e.,

$$\sum (\Delta t_0)^2 = (\Delta t_0^n)^2$$

$(\Delta t_0)^2 = (\Delta t_0^1)^2 + (\Delta t_0^2)^2 + (\Delta t_0^3)^2$
$(\Delta t_0)^2 = 2dt_0^1 . 2dt_0^1 + 2dt_0^2 . 2dt_0^2 + 2dt_0^3 . 2dt_0^3$

$$(\Delta t_0)^2 = \begin{vmatrix} 2dt_0^1 . 2dt_0^1 & 0 & 0 \\ 0 & 2dt_0^2 . 2dt_0^2 & 0 \\ 0 & 0 & 2dt_0^3 . 2dt_0^3 \end{vmatrix}$$

$$6dt_0 . 6dt_0 = \begin{vmatrix} 2dt_0^1 . 2dt_0^1 & 0 & 0 \\ 0 & 2dt_0^2 . 2dt_0^2 & 0 \\ 0 & 0 & 2dt_0^3 . 2dt_0^3 \end{vmatrix}$$

$6dt_0 . 6dt_0 = 2dt_0^1 . 2dt_0^1 + 2dt_0^2 . 2dt_0^2 + 2dt_0^3 . 2dt_0^3$

Therefore, Kāla Vyāpi Ālekha / Kāla Vyāpi Khaṇḍa dt_0 is equal to Kāla Vyāpi Khaṇḍa dt_0^1, dt_0^2 and dt_0^3.

२ Kāla Vyāpi Khaṇḍa of a Single Stem Asthira and Niṣiddha Kāla Vyāpi Ālekha

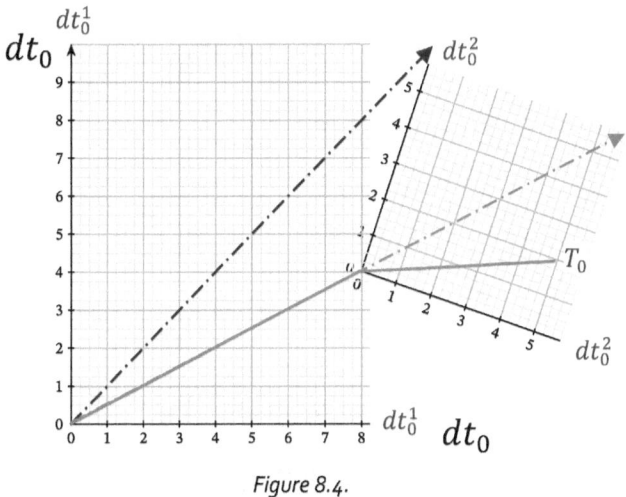

Figure 8.4.

This Kāla Vyāpi Ālekha depicts two states i.e., Asthira and Niṣiddha. Considering the Figure 8.4. where a Kāla Rekha T_0, for the Niṣiddha Kāla Vyāpi Ālekha dt_0, which has two origin points of which one is the Mūlādhāra with their respective Kāla Vyāpi Ālekha i.e., dt_0^1, dt_0^2 which are the Kāla Vyāpi Khaṇḍa. The Kāla Rekha T_0, can be calculated by diving the main Kāla Vyāpi Ālekha into two Kāla Vyāpi Khaṇḍa, which can be calculated separately as shown in the below figure.

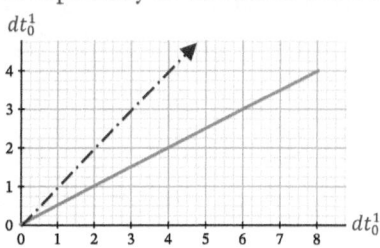

Kāla Vyāpi Khaṇḍa dt_0^1,

$$(\Delta t_0^1)^2 = \varkappa_0 dt_0^1 \cdot \varkappa_1 dt_0^1$$
$$(\Delta t_0^1)^2 = 8 dt_0^1 \cdot 4 dt_0^1$$

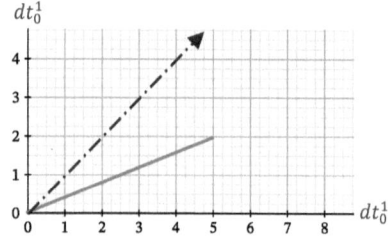

Kāla Vyāpi Khaṇḍa dt_0^2,

$$(\Delta t_0^1)^2 = \varkappa_0 dt_0^1 \cdot \varkappa_1 dt_0^1$$
$$(\Delta t_0^1)^2 = 5 dt_0^1 \cdot 2 dt_0^1$$

Kāla Vyāpi Khaṇḍa dt_0,

$$\sum_{i=1}^{m} (\Delta t_0)^2 = \varkappa_0 dt_0^i \cdot \varkappa_1 dt_0^i$$

$$\sum_{i=1}^{m=2} (\Delta t_0)^2 = \varkappa_0 dt_0^1 \cdot \varkappa_1 dt_0^1 + \varkappa_0 dt_0^2 \cdot \varkappa_1 dt_0^2$$

Here the upper limit of summation is 2, since we are considering only two Kāla Vyāpi Khaṇḍa i.e., dt_0^1 and dt_0^1.

Therefore, by substituting the 2 Kāla Vyāpi Khaṇḍa we get,

$$(\Delta t_0)^2 = \varkappa_0 dt_0 . \varkappa_1 dt_0 + \varkappa_0 dt_0 . \varkappa_1 dt_0$$
$$(\Delta t_0)^2 = 8dt_0 . 4dt_0 + 5dt_0 . 2dt_0$$
$$(\Delta t_0)^2 = \begin{vmatrix} 8dt_0 . 4dt_0 & 0 \\ 0 & 5dt_0 . 2dt_0 \end{vmatrix}$$

Now that we have got the Kāla Vyāpi Khaṇḍa dt_0, we now compare it with Kāla Vyāpi Khaṇḍa dt_0^1 and dt_0^1.

Hence we get,

$$\sum (\Delta t_0)^2 = (\Delta t_0^n)^2$$
$$(\Delta t_0)^2 = (\Delta t_0^1)^2 + (\Delta t_0^2)^2$$
$$(\Delta t_0)^2 = 8dt_0^1 . 4dt_0^1 + 5dt_0^2 . 2dt_0^2$$
$$(\Delta t_0)^2 = \begin{vmatrix} 8dt_0^1 . 4dt_0^1 & 0 \\ 0 & 5dt_0^2 . 2dt_0^2 \end{vmatrix}$$

$$\begin{vmatrix} 8dt_0 . 4dt_0 & 0 \\ 0 & 5dt_0 . 2dt_0 \end{vmatrix} = \begin{vmatrix} 8dt_0^1 . 4dt_0^1 & 0 \\ 0 & 5dt_0^2 . 2dt_0^2 \end{vmatrix}$$

$$8dt_0 . 4dt_0 + 5dt_0 . 2dt_0 = 8dt_0^1 . 4dt_0^1 + 5dt_0^2 . 2dt_0^2$$

Therefore, Kāla Vyāpi Ālekha / Kāla Vyāpi Khaṇḍa dt_0 is equal to Kāla Vyāpi Khaṇḍa dt_0^1 and dt_0^1.

Kāla Vyāpi Ālekha Saṅgraha

Kāla Vyāpi Ālekha Saṅgraha / Stack of Time Variant Graphs is a set of multiple Kāla Vyāpi Ālekha with same origin point or Mūlādhāra, which can also be considered as Branched Kāla Vyāpi Ālekha. These Branchings can be also considered as choices which are nothing but individual Kāla Rekha representing its Kāla Vyāpi Khaṇḍa. This Kāla Vyāpi Ālekha Saṅgraha can be further discriminated into the following types

१ Sthira Kāla Vyāpi Ālekha Saṅgraha

Representation of three different Single stem Sthira Kāla Vyāpi Ālekha i.e., dt_0, dt_1, dt_2 as Kāla Vyāpi Ālekha Saṅgraha / Stack of Time Variant Graph are as follows:

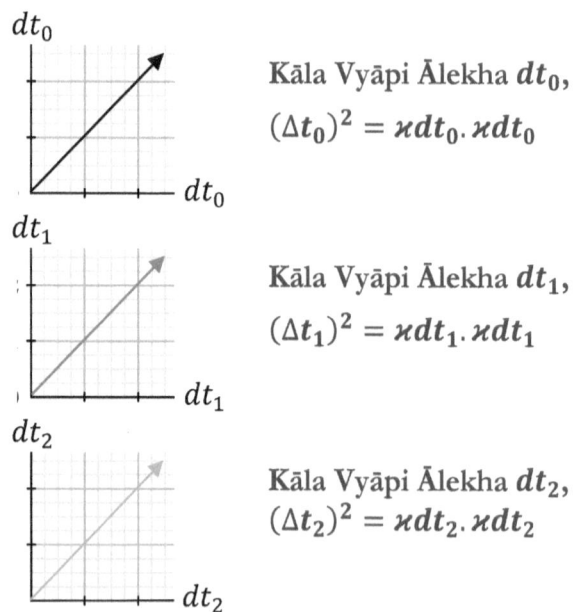

Kāla Vyāpi Ālekha dt_0,
$(\Delta t_0)^2 = \varkappa dt_0 . \varkappa dt_0$

Kāla Vyāpi Ālekha dt_1,
$(\Delta t_1)^2 = \varkappa dt_1 . \varkappa dt_1$

Kāla Vyāpi Ālekha dt_2,
$(\Delta t_2)^2 = \varkappa dt_2 . \varkappa dt_2$

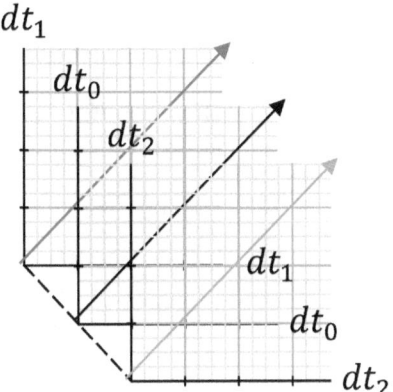

Sthira Kāla Vyāpi Ālekha Saṅgraha

$$\left(\Delta t_{0,1,2}\right)^2 = \begin{vmatrix} (\Delta t_0)^2 & 0 & 0 \\ 0 & (\Delta t_1)^2 & 0 \\ 0 & 0 & (\Delta t_2)^2 \end{vmatrix}$$

$$\left(\Delta t_{0,1,2}\right)^2 = \begin{vmatrix} \varkappa dt_0.\varkappa dt_0 & 0 & 0 \\ 0 & \varkappa dt_1.\varkappa dt_1 & 0 \\ 0 & 0 & \varkappa dt_2.\varkappa dt_2 \end{vmatrix}$$

२ **Asthira Kāla Vyāpi Ālekha Saṅgraha**

Representation of three different Single Stem Asthira Kāla Vyāpi Ālekha i.e., dt_0, dt_1, dt_2 as Kāla Vyāpi Ālekha Saṅgraha / Stack of Time Variant Graph are as follows:

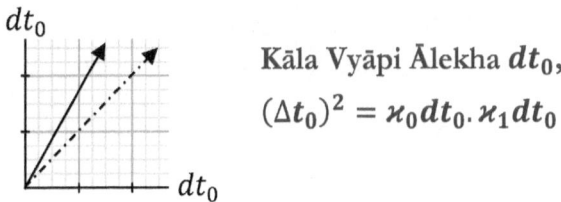

Kāla Vyāpi Ālekha dt_0,

$(\Delta t_0)^2 = \varkappa_0 dt_0.\varkappa_1 dt_0$

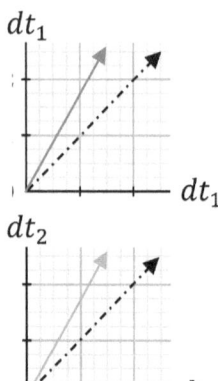

Kāla Vyāpi Ālekha dt_1,
$(\Delta t_1)^2 = \varkappa_0 dt_1 . \varkappa_1 dt_1$

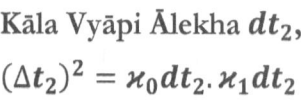

Kāla Vyāpi Ālekha dt_2,
$(\Delta t_2)^2 = \varkappa_0 dt_2 . \varkappa_1 dt_2$

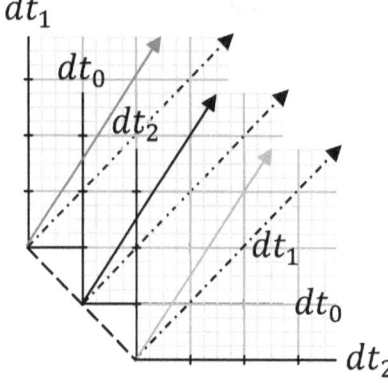

Asthira Kāla Vyāpi Ālekha Saṅgraha

$$\left(\Delta t_{0,1,2}\right)^2 = \begin{vmatrix} (\Delta t_0)^2 & 0 & 0 \\ 0 & (\Delta t_1)^2 & 0 \\ 0 & 0 & (\Delta t_2)^2 \end{vmatrix}$$

$$\left(\Delta t_{0,1,2}\right)^2 = \begin{vmatrix} \varkappa_0 dt_0 . \varkappa_1 dt_0 & 0 & 0 \\ 0 & \varkappa_0 dt_1 . \varkappa_1 dt_1 & 0 \\ 0 & 0 & \varkappa_0 dt_2 . \varkappa_1 dt_2 \end{vmatrix}$$

3 Niṣiddha Kāla Vyāpi Ālekha Saṅgraha

Representation of three different Niṣiddha Kāla Vyāpi Ālekha i.e., dt_0, dt_1, dt_2 as Kāla Vyāpi Ālekha Saṅgraha / Stack of Time Variant Graph are as follows

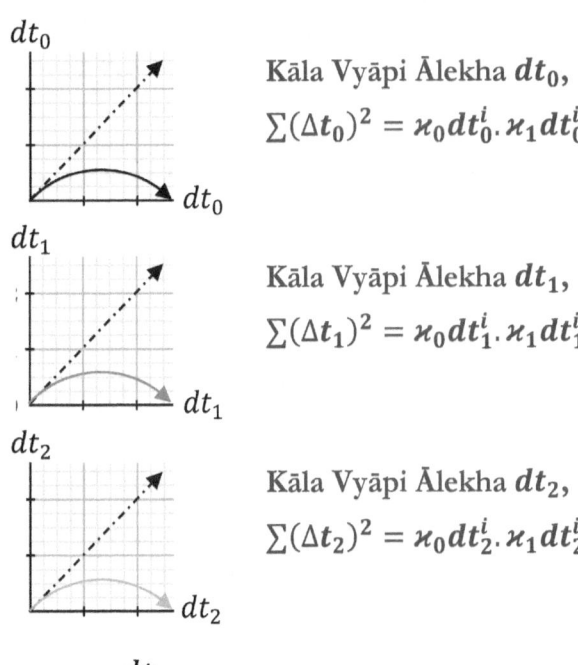

Kāla Vyāpi Ālekha dt_0,
$$\sum (\Delta t_0)^2 = \varkappa_0 dt_0^i . \varkappa_1 dt_0^i$$

Kāla Vyāpi Ālekha dt_1,
$$\sum (\Delta t_1)^2 = \varkappa_0 dt_1^i . \varkappa_1 dt_1^i$$

Kāla Vyāpi Ālekha dt_2,
$$\sum (\Delta t_2)^2 = \varkappa_0 dt_2^i . \varkappa_1 dt_2^i$$

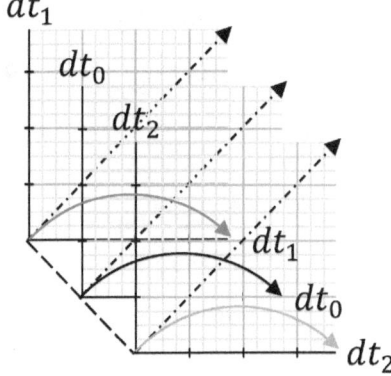

Niṣiddha Kāla Vyāpi Ālekha Saṅgraha

$$\left(\Delta t_{0,1,2}\right)^2 = \begin{vmatrix} \sum(\Delta t_0)^2 & 0 & 0 \\ 0 & \sum(\Delta t_1)^2 & 0 \\ 0 & 0 & \sum(\Delta t_2)^2 \end{vmatrix}$$

$$\left(\Delta t_{0,1,2}\right)^2 = \begin{vmatrix} \sum\left(\varkappa_0 dt_0^i \cdot \varkappa_1 dt_0^i\right) & 0 & 0 \\ 0 & \sum\left(\varkappa_0 dt_0^i \cdot \varkappa_1 dt_0^i\right) & 0 \\ 0 & 0 & \sum\left(\varkappa_0 dt_0^i \cdot \varkappa_1 dt_0^i\right) \end{vmatrix}$$

8 Kāla Vyāpi Khaṇḍa and Kāla Vyāpi Ālekha Saṅgraha for Sthira Kāla Vyāpi Ālekha

Considering a Branched Kāla Vyāpi Ālekha where there are two Kāla Vyāpi Khaṇḍa i.e., dt_0^1, dt_0^2, of which dt_0^2 has a Kāla Vyāpi Ālekha saṅgraha i.e., dt_0^2, dt_1^2, dt_2^2 respectively as shown in the Figure 8.5

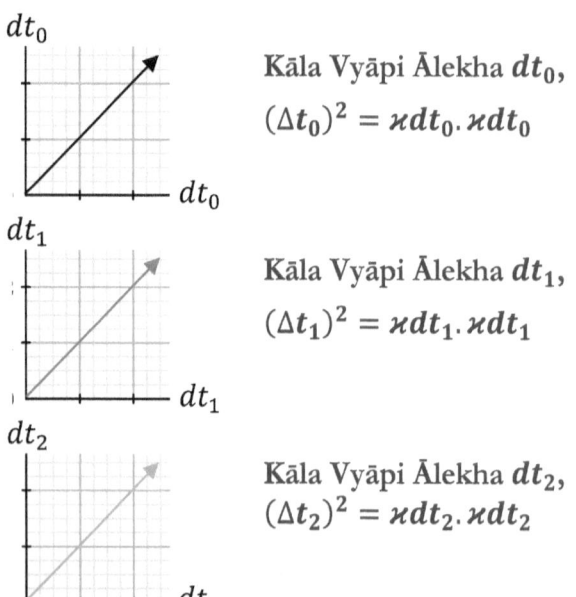

Kāla Vyāpi Ālekha dt_0,
$(\Delta t_0)^2 = \varkappa dt_0 \cdot \varkappa dt_0$

Kāla Vyāpi Ālekha dt_1,
$(\Delta t_1)^2 = \varkappa dt_1 \cdot \varkappa dt_1$

Kāla Vyāpi Ālekha dt_2,
$(\Delta t_2)^2 = \varkappa dt_2 \cdot \varkappa dt_2$

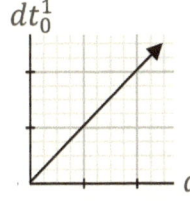

Kāla Vyāpi Khaṇḍa dt_0^1,

$$\left(\Delta t_0^1\right)^2 = \varkappa dt_0^1 \cdot \varkappa dt_0^1$$

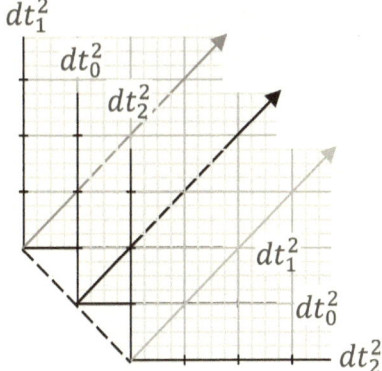

Kāla Vyāpi Ālekha Saṅgraha

$$\left(\Delta t_{0,1,2}^2\right)^2 = \begin{vmatrix} (\Delta t_0^2)^2 & 0 & 0 \\ 0 & (\Delta t_1^2)^2 & 0 \\ 0 & 0 & (\Delta t_2^2)^2 \end{vmatrix}$$

$$\left(\Delta t_{0,1,2}^2\right)^2 = \begin{vmatrix} \varkappa dt_0^2 \cdot \varkappa dt_0^2 & 0 & 0 \\ 0 & \varkappa dt_1^2 \cdot \varkappa dt_1^2 & 0 \\ 0 & 0 & \varkappa dt_2^2 \cdot \varkappa dt_2^2 \end{vmatrix}$$

Kāla Siddhānta

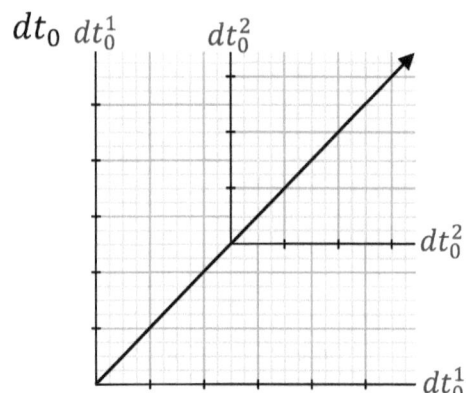

Kāla Vyāpi Khaṇḍa for dt_0,

$$(\Delta t_0)^2 = \begin{vmatrix} \left(\Delta t_0^1\right)^2 & 0 \\ 0 & \left(\Delta t_0^2\right)^2 \end{vmatrix}$$

$$(\Delta t_0)^2 = \begin{vmatrix} \varkappa dt_0^1 \cdot \varkappa dt_0^1 & 0 \\ 0 & \varkappa dt_0^2 \cdot \varkappa dt_0^2 \end{vmatrix}$$

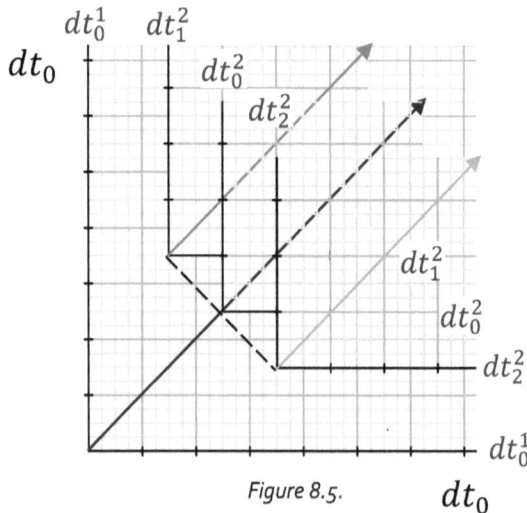

Figure 8.5.

Final Kāla Vyāpi Ālekha Sangraha and Khaṇḍa for dt_0,

$$(\Delta t_0)^2 = \begin{vmatrix} (\Delta t_0^1)^2 & 0 \\ 0 & (\Delta t_0^2)^2 \end{vmatrix}$$

Substituting Kāla Vyāpi Sangraha at Δt_0^2,

$$(\Delta t_0)^2 = \begin{vmatrix} (\Delta t_0^1)^2 & 0 \\ 0 & \left(\Delta t_{0,1,2}^2\right)^2 \end{vmatrix}$$

$$(\Delta t_0)^2 = \begin{vmatrix} (\Delta t_0^1)^2 & 0 \\ 0 & \begin{vmatrix} (\Delta t_0^2)^2 & 0 & 0 \\ 0 & (\Delta t_1^2)^2 & 0 \\ 0 & 0 & (\Delta t_2^2)^2 \end{vmatrix} \end{vmatrix}$$

$$(\Delta t_0)^2 = \begin{vmatrix} \varkappa dt_0^1 . \varkappa dt_0^1 & 0 \\ 0 & \begin{vmatrix} \varkappa dt_0^2 . \varkappa dt_0^2 & 0 & 0 \\ 0 & \varkappa dt_1^2 . \varkappa dt_1^2 & 0 \\ 0 & 0 & \varkappa dt_2^2 . \varkappa dt_2^2 \end{vmatrix} \end{vmatrix}$$

- **Saṃyoga Kāla Rekha**

When two individual Kāla Rekha merge, they form a new Kāla Rekha i.e., Saṁyoga Kāla Rekha / The Merged Timeline. This merging of Kāla Rekha can be discriminated into two types.

१ Kāla Rekha Saṃkalana

Kāla Rekha Saṃkalana / Addition of Kāla Rekha, where this newly formed Kāla Rekha is the product of the two Merged Kāla Rekha. Here, when we consider the following Kāla Rekha T_1 and T_2, the Saṃkalanam of those Kāla Rekha will be a Saṁyoga Kāla Rekha i.e., T_3 as shown in the Figure 8.6.

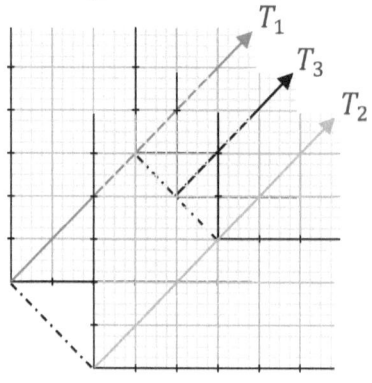

Figure 8.6.

$$T_1 + T_2 = T_3$$

२ Kāla Rekha Vyavakalana

Kāla Rekha Vyavakalana / Division of Kāla Rekha, where a Saṁyoga Kāla Rekha is divided into multiple Kāla Rekha. Here, when we consider the following Kāla Rekha T_1 and T_2, the Saṃkalanam of those Kāla Rekha will be a Saṁyoga Kāla Rekha i.e., T_3, which will again split up into T_1 and T_2, and may also branch into many other Kāla Rekha as shown in the Figure 8.7.

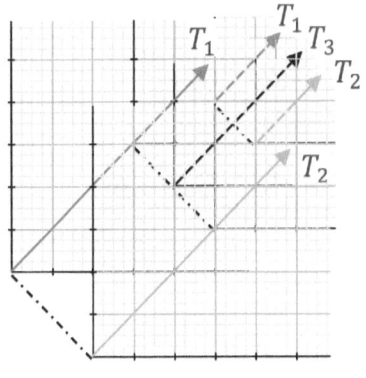

Figure 8.7.

$$T_3 = T_1 + T_2$$

- **Prabhāvita Kāla Rekha**

Prabhāvita Kāla Rekha / Influential Timeline, the name itself says that these are influential Kāla Rekha. The Saṁyoga Kāla Rekha is a new Kāla Rekha that is formed and is highly influenced by both the individual Kāla Rekha that have been merged and will share their characteristics, where each of the individual Kāla Rekha that have merged will influence the future of this Saṁyoga Kāla Rekha. Every Kāla Rekha may not be an influential Kāla Rekha, but every Saṁyoga Kāla Rekha is an influential Kāla Rekha. Due to which, disturbing these Kāla Rekha will lead to catastrophe. For example, if a Kāla Rekha ends before it's predicted ending, then it will not give rise to another Influential Kāla Rekha which will not give rise to another and so on. Therefore, if continues to happen then there will be an empty void in Kāla and disrupt the further predestined outcomes of the Kāla Rekha.

▪ Kāla Rekha Samāptaṃ

As we already know that a Kāla Rekha depends on the object, so does the end of it. A Kāla Rekha that originates from singularity i.e., the Mūlādhāra, has an indefinite ending, or in other words we can say that the object bounded by its Kāla Sūtra has an indefinite ending. Although the end is indefinite but is inevitable.

▪ Samāptaṃ of Single Stem Kāla Vyāpi Ālekha

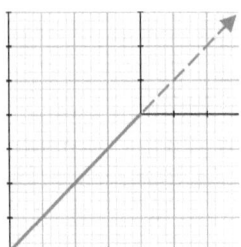

Figure 8.8: Illustration of Single Stem Sthira Kāla Vyāpi Ālekha

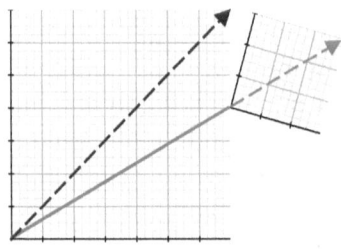

Figure 8.9: Illustration of Single Stem Asthira Kāla Vyāpi Ālekha

Kāla Rekha of a Single Stem Sthira and Asthira Kāla Vyāpi Ālekha starts from the Mūlādhāra, which can also be considered as the First Kāla Vyāpi Khaṇḍa and ends at its Last Kāla Vyāpi Khaṇḍa as shown in the above Figures 8.8 and 9.

- **Samāptaṃ of Branched Kāla Vyāpi Ālekha**
A branched Kāla Vyāpi Ālekha which arise form a single or a common Kāla Vyāpi Khaṇḍa can end in multiple ways, of which some can be predicted and some not. These endings can be mainly of two types, which are explained below.

१ **Samāna Samāptaṃ of Branched Kāla Vyāpi Ālekha**

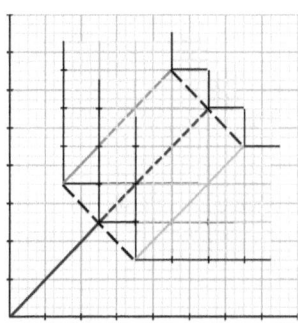 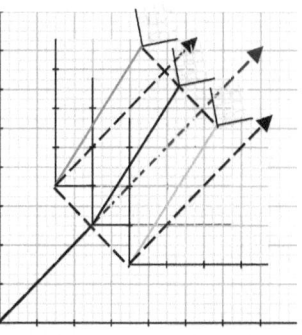

Figure 8.10: Illustration of Branched Sthira Kāla Vyāpi Ālekha

Figure 8.11: Illustration of Branched Asthira Kāla Vyāpi Ālekha

Kāla Rekha of a Single Stem Sthira and Asthira Kāla Vyāpi Ālekha starts from the Mūlādhāra, which can also be considered as the First Kāla Vyāpi Khaṇḍa which later on splits to form a Branched Sthira and Asthira Kāla Vyāpi Ālekha at a specific Kāla Vyāpi Khaṇḍa. Where, further all the Kāla Rekha in the Branched Sthira and Asthira Kāla Vyāpi Ālekha end at the same Kāla Vyāpi Khaṇḍa, as shown in the above Figures 8.10 and 8.11.

२ Asamāna Samāptaṃ of Branched Kāla Vyāpi Ālekha

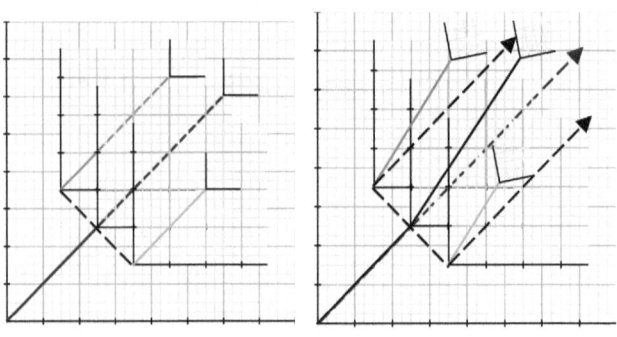

Figure 8.12: Illustration of Branched Sthira Kāla Vyāpi Ālekha

Figure 8.13: Illustration of Branched Asthira Kāla Vyāpi Ālekha

Kāla Rekha of a Single Stem Sthira and Asthira Kāla Vyāpi Ālekha starts from the Mūlādhāra, which can also be considered as the First Kāla Vyāpi Khaṇḍa which later on splits to form a Branched Sthira and Asthira Kāla Vyāpi Ālekha at a specific Kāla Vyāpi

Khaṇḍa. Where, further all the Kāla Rekha in the Branched Sthira and Asthira Kāla Vyāpi Ālekha end at different Kāla Vyāpi Khaṇḍa, as shown in the above Figures 8.12 and 8.13.

MAHAKĀLA

The Multiverse is a subject that we know very little about, where as of now what we know about our universe is nothing, and we are trying to figure out about the multiverses. Multiverses are often considered as many universes as possible, co-existing together in harmony where we have an assumption of $10^{10^{10^{24}}}$ universes. Here no one knows what is this Multiverse, how do they affect each other, how are these co-existing or is this even real? Real, realism, reality, these words express submissiveness in its own form, which predetermines the very existence from maya to reality. What would have been if there would not have been any such word as reality or any synonym of it. What we call as reality would have been completely different of what we know now.

- ## MahaKāla

After clearing the doubt of Kāla Rekha, let's travel the multiverse. As of today, we might have made a boundary in space called as our universe in which we all live, yet we are not sure that there is a boundary to our universe. All we know that this is an expanding universe as, something happened in the center long back which caused this existence, "The Big Bang" they say. So, some people came up with a thought of multiple universes on the same basis of multiple big bangs in space. Imagine multiple big bangs happening randomly in space at multiple times, giving rise to multiple universes.

Here, basically Multiverse means multiple universes. Where it clearly states that different universes rather than ours, which may or may not have our planet earth. Even if the earth existed, would it have looked the way we know it? would there have been any life form? Would there have been the great human race? If yes, then would the humans have looked the same and have the same traits? There can be endless different possibilities and assumptions.

MahaKāla means the most supreme Kāla, and as already mentioned Kāla not only means Time but even space so this MahaKāla is consider as the ultimate supremacy of existence of anything that can be possibly imagined, defined, or comprehended. This MahaKāla holds and sustains the existence of all the multiple universes in it. This can further be descried in two aspects / features.

१ Kālāntara Kāla Rekha (Inter-universal Kāla Rekha)

A universe consists of multiple of objects, which can be stars, black holes, supernovas, planets, and its multiple life forms. Where we know that each of these objects have their own Kāla Rekha. Therefore, these multiple objects and Kāla Rekha, for a single universe, can be considered as Kālāntara Kāla Rekha / Inter-

Universal Kāla Rekha. All that we have known about Kāla Rekha come under this part. Hence, each individual Universe means **Kāla** in its own perspective and the objects with its Kāla Rekha are **Kālāntara Kāla Rekha**. Kāla (universe) consists of multiple branched Kāla Rekha arising from Mūlādhāra, where these branched Kāla Rekha can be considered singularly as Kālāntara Kāla Rekha.

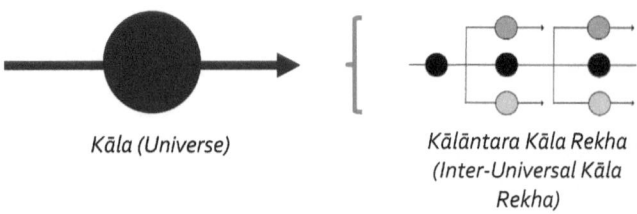

Kāla (Universe)   Kālāntara Kāla Rekha (Inter-Universal Kāla Rekha)

Figure 9.1: Illustration of Kālāntara Kāla Rekha

2. MahaKālāntara Kāla Rekha (Multiversal Kāla Rekha)

MahaKāla consists of multiple universes i.e., Multiverse, and each universe in this, possesses its uniqueness which has its own Kāla Rekha called as MahaKālāntara Kāla Rekha. Here, Multiverse means **MahaKāla** and the multiple universes with its respective Kāla Rekha inside the Multiverse are called as MahaKālāntara Kāla Rekha / Multiversal Kāla Rekha. Each universe in the multiverse as its own Mūlādhāra and Mūlā Kāla Rekha or main Kāla Rekha.

MahaKālāntara Kāla Rekha

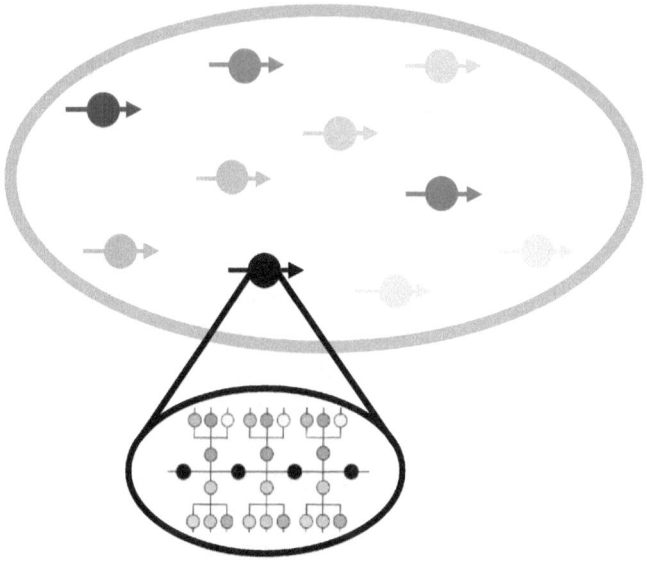

Figure 9.2: Illustration of MahaKālāntara Kāla Rekha

The Figure 9.2. illustrates MahaKāla, where each colored circle signifies and stands for the uniqueness of a single universe (Kāla) and its Kāla Rekha as an arrow passing through it. These collections of universes (Kāla) are called as MahaKāla, and each universe's Kāla Rekha is called as MahaKālāntara Kāla Rekha.

KĀLA REKHA ANUNĀDAḤ

"If you want to find the secrets of the universe, think in terms of energy, frequency and vibration."

-- Nikola Tesla

One of the great scientists of our Timeline, Nikola Tesla commenting these words as his life's work is a gift to the mankind, which includes great inventions and beautiful theories. **Anunādaḥ** means Resonance in Sanskrit which a beautiful, but yet quite terrifying phenomena. This concept postulates that everything has its own vibration i.e., natural frequency, which can come in sync when perfectly matched by an external (artificial) frequency. Tesla's magic frequency, when two input frequencies of which one should be 11 Times of the lower frequency. When done both the objects resonate, and as we increase the frequency, the natural frequency of the object gets altered and the object is destroyed. This very phenomenon was responsible for causing an earthquake back in 1893, by an electro-mechanical oscillator, a steam powered electric generator patented by Nikola Tesla. On pondering this, I wonder whether these timelines also have their own natural frequencies, and if so, can it be observed and controlled?

▪ Kāla Rekha Anunādaḥ

Imagine if we could communicate with a different Kāla Rekha, an Kālāntara Kāla Rekha / Inter-universal Kāla Rekha, maybe even with a MahaKālāntara Kāla Rekha / Multiversal Kāla Rekha. Just like how we communicate by phone calls and internet, only here if we could communicate by using the resonance of the Kāla Rekha. Why are we considering the Kāla Rekha's resonance? The answer is simple and is in the early chapters of this work, i.e., when we consider Kāla Rekha, which are nothing but Asthira Kāla Sūtra / Disturbed Strings of Time, and anything that is being disturbed is being oscillated and hence it is in vibration, that is nothing but its natural frequency. Therefore, each Kāla Rekha being unique will have its own unique resonating frequency.

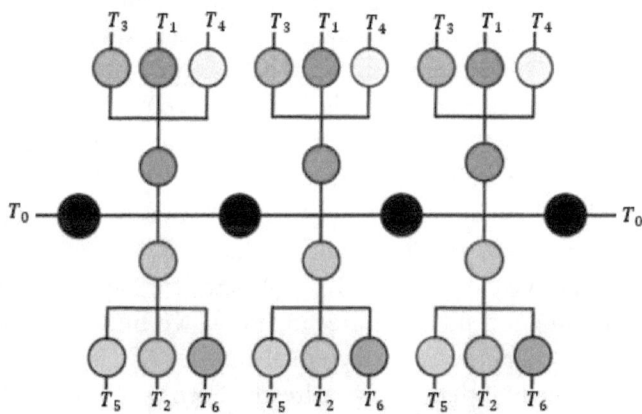

Figure 10.1: Illustration of a Branched Kāla Rekha

Considering a branched Kāla Rekha and its typical features as show in the above Figure 10.1. Here in this Kāla Rekha flow chart, we can see multiple Kāla Rekha represented with the same Nāmakaraṇa (names). Where we also observe a pattern in this branched Kāla Rekha. Therefore, the collection of these same named Kāla Rekha will have the same natural frequency and resonate in synchronization. Here this resonance means transfer or exchange of information between the Kāla Rekha. When either of the Kāla Rekha which might have had started early or after likewise, are considered as relative to each other. But as soon as there will be a match among the frequencies of these same named Kāla Rekha the exchange of information between the Kāla Rekha is initiated. This 'matching of frequencies' can be considered as an event which are nothing but the same superposition of choice which has been selected in an alternate Kāla Rekha. This transfer of information can be of the information about the respective Kāla Rekha's events that have already happened or are yet to happen in either of the Kāla Rekha. When we consider a simple branched Kāla Rekha flow chart, the resonance between the Kāla Rekha can be predicted and is illustrated as shown in the above Figure 10.1. When we apply this phenomenon into real life situations, we find that this is being experienced for a small amount of Time. This eerie feeling that you've already been here or have already done this before can be considered as a best example of the exchange of information between our respective alternate Kāla Rekha. Where this feeling of

'Déjà vu', can be consider as an information from an alternate Kāla Rekha. When a person's superpositional choice from this and alternate Kāla Rekha match, both the Kāla Rekha start resonating in the same frequency initiating a surg of information. This is a two-way transfer, where one is experiencing the surge of information the same happens on the other resonating Kāla Rekha as well. Some information i.e., events from both sides of the Kāla Rekha are being exchanged.

Here for example, considering Kāla Rekha t_1 and t_2.

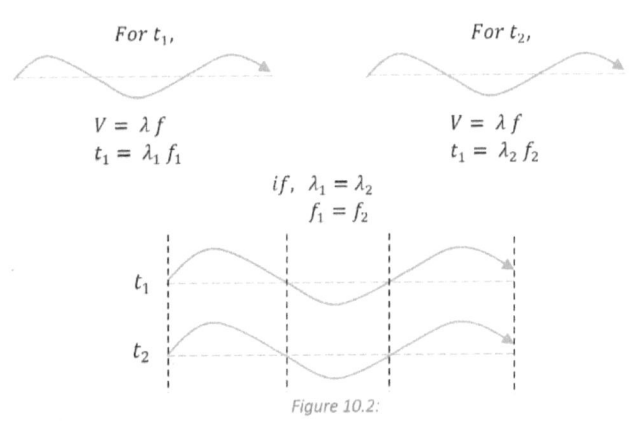

Figure 10.2:

When the wavelength and the frequency of both the Kāla Rekha match, the Kāla Rekha come in perfect sync, which will result in alignment of the Kāla Rekha which is very crucial for this conjecture, then there will be exchange of information between the Kāla Rekha. As shown in the Figure 10.2. The exchange of information between the Kāla Rekha can be, knowing about the other Kāla Rekha features. When these Kāla Rekha are in perfect sync, there might be even possibility of jumping through Kāla Rekha at any synchronized point.

KĀLA SAMKRAMAṆAM

Samkramaṇam means Transition in Sanskrit, of which here it is referred to as Time Travelling which is a subject of fantasy and excitement which comes with its own risks. This is that topic which is supposed to be understood less and is often quite misunderstood. There have been many misconceptions over the centuries due to many movies, fantasies, theories, and paradoxes, which has led to many questions and less conclusions.

As we already know that each Asthira Kāla Rekha has all three states of Trikālagyana, where these states are nothing but one's point of perspective of understanding an Kāla Rekha, which can be represented as shown in the Figure 11.1. below.

Figure 11.1: Illustration of Trikālagyana on a Kāla Rekha

Considering the above Figure 11.1. depicting a Kāla Rekha, where a point of perspective on a Kāla Rekha determines the states of Trikālagyana, which is seen in two perspectives as shown in the above figure. In the 1st perspective, we considered a point on the Kāla Rekha and name the states of Trikālagyana Accordingly, Bhūta, Vartamāna and Bhaviśya.

Therefore, as we move along the Kāla Rekha i.e., when we overcome the Vartamāna Kāla and move on to the next i.e., Bhaviśya Kāla, this Bhaviśya Kāla will now become the Vartamāna Kāla and the previous Vartamāna Kāla will become the Bhūta Kāla of the 2nd perspective as shown in the Figure 11.1, this continues so on according to one's perspective. Hence the Kāla Rekha and its respective States of Trikālagyana are predefined, where the observer or object moves through Kāla Rekha, and not that Kāla Rekha that moves through or along the observer or object.

- **Kāla Saṁkramaṇam / Time Transition**

The actual displacement of an object from anynamed point 'A' to point 'B' on a Kāla Rekha T_0 is called Kāla Saṁkramaṇam. The proper flow of Kāla is considered as the actual displacement of a Kāla Rekha as the basic and natural Kāla Saṁkramaṇam.

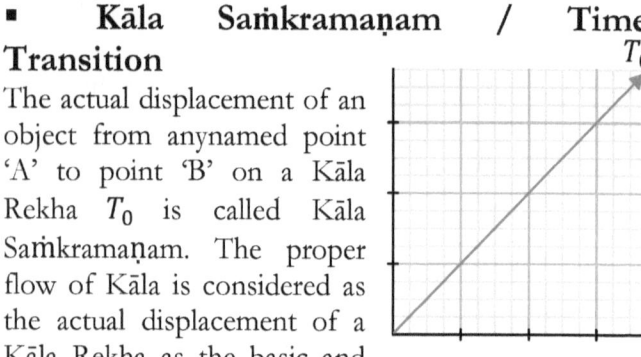

Figure 11.2:

There are two types of Kāla Saṁkramaṇam:

१ Bhūta Kāla Saṁkramaṇam.
२ Bhaviśya Kāla Saṁkramaṇam.

९ Bhūta Kāla Saṁkramaṇam

The adjunct displacement of an object from point 'A' Vartamāna Kāla to point 'B' Bhūta Kāla on a Kāla Rekha T_0 is called Bhūta Kāla Saṁkramaṇam. Here, we consider a Kāla Rekha T_0 as MūlāKāla Rekha which has its basic Kāla Vyāpi Ālekha features.

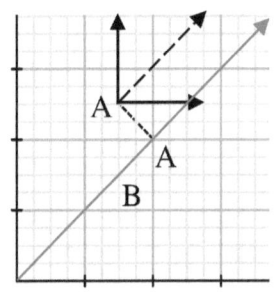

Figure 11.3:

Point 'A' on the MūlāKāla Rekha is a branched Kāla Rekha which initiates Kāla Saṁkramaṇam to point 'B' as shown in the Figure 11.3. Since we already know that we can't travel backwards in Time or in Kāla Rekha, so traveling to point 'B' from 'A' is achievable with the help of Asthira and Niṣiddha Kāla Vyāpi Rekha.

A series of we calibrated Asthira Kāla Vyāpi Rekha from point 'A', branch to form a curve or a loop to reach and connect point 'B' as shown in the Figure 11.4. From point 'A', an Asthira Kāla Vyāpi Rekha branches, which continues for a specific period and another Asthira Kāla Vyāpi Rekha branches from it and so on. Here multiple Asthira Kāla Vyāpi Rekha' branch and lie in their respective Kāla Vyāpi Ālekha or Londe manifold, where they form a Asthira Kāla Vyāpi Ālekha Saṅgraha. This series of Asthira Kāla Vyāpi Rekha can also be considered as Niṣiddha Kāla Vyāpi Rekha, where these series of Kāla Rekha must not exceed beyond the Kāla Vyāpi Sīmā.

Kāla Siddhānta

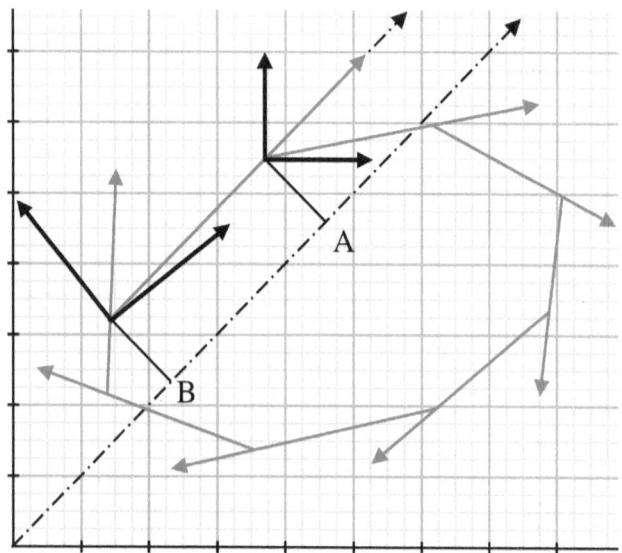

Figure 11.4: Illustration of Bhūta Kāla Saṁkramaṇam

Here, this complex Kāla Vyāpi Ālekha can be represented in a simplified form where the multiple Asthira Kāla Vyāpi Ālekha can be represented in the form of a loop which makes it easy to illustrate and visualize. This Kāla Saṁkramaṇam also come with its own risks, where an infinite spiral may be caused in the Kāla Vyāpi Ālekha, which keeps on branching into a series of unstable Kāla Vyāpi Ālekha. Where it makes it look like an infinite spiral in the Londe manifold consisting of Kāla Vyāpi Saṅgraha. This is caused due the lack of Bhūta Kāla i.e., point 'B' on the MūlāKāla Rekha T_0.

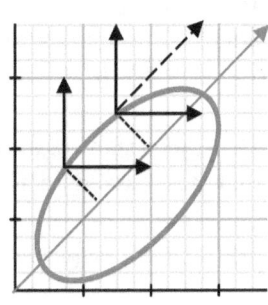
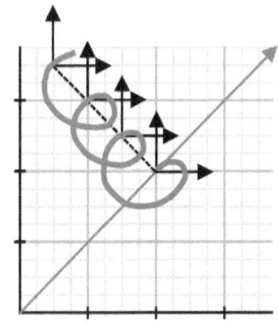

Figure 11.5:   *Figure 11.6:*

२   **Bhaviṣya Kāla Saṁkramaṇam**

This can simply be considered as the actual displacement of an object, from point 'A' Vartamāna Kāla to point 'B' Bhaviṣya Kāla as shown in the Figure 11.6. Where this Bhaviṣya Kāla Saṁkramaṇam can be considered as natural Kāla Saṁkramaṇam, as there is no other way to transit to the Bhaviṣya Kāla better than this, and that we already are transitioning into Bhaviṣya Kāla.

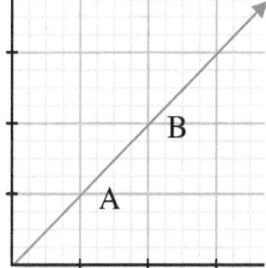

Figure 11.6:

- **Kāla Saṁkramaṇam Doṣa**

१ Here the important points to remember are that, when try to loop in Time to go before Time, Time is needed for Time Traveling.

२ When traveling back in Time, we might require more Time than actual Time that has passed in the respective Kāla Rekha.

३ We just cannot go back to the Time, where we started the journey of Time.

४ We can only go back in Time or stay in the loop.

५ Once looped we can further create new choice which will affect the outcome of the respective Kāla Rekha.

६ When we travel back in Time, that past become our new future.

KĀLA REKHA ŚĀSTRA

Śāstras, In Sanskrit rules are called as Śāstras. Rules are a set of regulations or principle that govern or conduct within a particular area of activity. Here our area of activity is Kāla, which is not quite simple. Nothing is simple when it is associated with Kāla. These set of rules or Śāstras, will govern the Kāla Rekha. The whole book has been a part where we have been dealing with rules and warnings associated with Time where even a slight mistake definitely leads to catastrophe. These rules will be the foundations of what's coming and what has already happened. These rules are not supposed to be neglected and to be followed seriously. As of now, to our basic knowledge of the rules of Kālāntara and MahaKālāntara Kāla Rekha, knowingly or unknowingly have being obeyed. Though we have come to the end of this concept, there yet remains a lot to know about Kāla. As far as we have been, we have only known basic structure, behavior, types, and characteristics of the Kāla Rekha. Yet we lack the knowledge of the functionality of the Kāla Rekha.

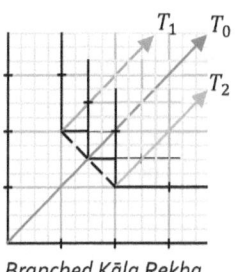

Branched Kāla Rekha

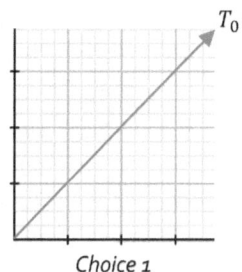

Choice 1

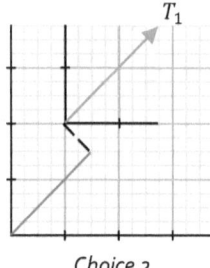
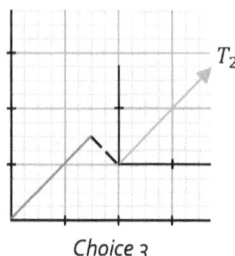

Figure 12.1:

Now the pondered question 'how a Kāla Rekha works?' Will be resolved through life situations / references. Considering a simple Branched Kāla Rekha with three branches, which represent three choices. These three choices are the Kāla Rekha T_0, T_1 and T_2, where T_0 is the MūlāKāla Rekha. Kāla Rekha T_1 and T_2 are the branches of T_0 which is the MūlāKāla Rekha, and it lies in a Superposition. To maintain the proper flow of Time, one choice is chosen out of three which collapses the superposition to a single outcome. This may look simple, but this is where the concept gets trickier. The three choices when chosen separately, splits up into 3 different realities. As we cans see in the Figure 12.1, Choice 1: where Kāla Rekha T_0 is chosen, Choice 2: where Kāla Rekha T_1 is chosen and Choice 3: where Kāla Rekha T_3 is chosen. Here among three choices when one is chosen, the superposition collapses to a single outcome and the other choices become nil or which cannot be chosen again in this Kāla Rekha / Timeline. Those other remaining choices are chosen in a different Kāla Rekha / Timeline predetermining that Kāla Rekha's reality.

Consider a thought experiment, where right now you are reading this book and say you also have two choices, either stop reading this book and do something else or to continue reading. Right now, at this very moment you have become the object of reference for the Asthira Kāla Sutra around you, and this is your Asthira Kāla Rekha, which currently lies in a superposition waiting to collapse to a single outcome to determine your realty and predict your future. All that is left for you is to choose, one choice. As soon you make a choice at that very moment your Kāla Rekha splits into two different Kāla Rekha of which one is the choice that you made right now. But what if I told you that the other Kāla Rekha also exits parallelly, and that you have chosen the other choice in that Kāla Rekha. Say for example, you choose to read the book, the other choice of not reading it also exist parallelly. Even though you are reading this very sentence right now, you are also doing something else in another Kāla Rekha. Therefore, both the choices are chosen in their respective Kala Rekha, and this cannot be changed. Therefore, this above explanation perfectly describes the first line of the shloka given below where, no matter what choice is made out of many, all the other choices are made in their respective Kāla Rekha / Timeline predetermining its respective reality.

यत् भवितव्यं तत् भवन्तः कियत् अपि परिवर्तयितुं प्रयतन्ते चेदपि भविष्यति |

यदि च भवन्तः मन्यन्ते यत् भवन्तः यत् भवितव्यम् आसीत् तत् परिवर्तितम् तर्हि तत् एव भवितव्यम् आसीत् ||1||

What has to happen will happen no matter how hard you try to change it.

And if you think you have changed, what was supposed to happen, then that is what was supposed to happen.

Coming to the second line of the shloka where, even though one choice is made, and all the other choice happens in their own respective Kāla Rekha. Where one feels that he has a certain predefined choice which is yet to happen and thinks that he can change the reality by choosing a different choice. But that is not how Kāla Rekha works. Though he might think that he can change the Kāla Rekha by choosing a different choice, and makes the other choice, then that was the choice that was supposed to be chosen. Thus, the second line of the shloka is described. Overall, what is happening is happing due to the pious nature of Kāla and is in proper way. This should not be altered or interfered by any means.

एकदा कृतं न कर्तुं शक्यते तथा च दैवं पूर्णं कर्तव्यम् ।
ज्ञात्वा कालं न दानं तु ज्ञानशापम् ।।2।।

Once done cannot be undone and Destiny has to be fulfilled.

Knowing Time is not a gift but a curse, a curse of knowledge.

'WHAT IF', a powerful statement consisting of two simple words, which can make something meaningful and also meaningless. Though being such a powerful statement it's better that it remains as a hypothetical statement. Many statements can be stated using these words, but the ones regarding this work, sometimes makes me stay up all night. **What if** these rules are not followed? As told earlier, this is not just a theory but guide, a procedure to maintain the proper flow of Kāla/Time, a rule book which has to be followed to maintain the sanity of this Kāla Rekha/Timeline.

The above shloka doesn't need any explanation where the first line clearly states that once done cannot be on done, which even implies to the Kāla Saṁkramaṇam / Time Transition concept where if we go back in time and change the course of Kāla Rekha and its reality by choosing other choices, then this changed Kāla Rekha is not the same Kāla Rekha that it was before but a new branch which was also supposed to happen, and the destiny of creation of this Kāla Rekha had to be fulfilled. Where at this point it becomes completely obvious that everything is predefined. Me publishing this very book, to you buying it and reading it till this very moment, to yet other things to come and happen. Even though we have choices that can be chosen the outcomes are predefined and that is the **Truth**.

Thus but no further, the very last line of the above shloka describes this knowledge in a very disturbing way, where knowing Kāla / Time is not a gift but curse to know and to live with. I could never express my experience of this journey through Time, in course of drafting this book where the horrors I have seen are beyond one's comprehension, things which have happened to me personally and are yet to happen to me and to the humankind. By this I conclude this work on Time i.e., **Kāla Siddhānta** by quoting.

YOU WILL LIVE TO SEE MAN-MADE HORRORS BEYOND YOUR COMPREHENSION.

- TESLA

ADHYĀY-3

PARADOXES AND MYTHS

Here in this phase, we completely reconsider the basic principles of physics and not just blindly follow them based on some mathematically despicable relation. Here the only relation is between us and our thought. As the Aristotle tradition says one can govern the laws of physics just by pure thought.

- ### The Kālashri Paradox

For the past centuries and Millenniums, there have been many theories on Time. But it is often said that Time is cyclic in many old scriptures, at least in Hinduism. It is said that this is the 14th creation, and these events keep on repeating over and over again. To me personally, I do not consider Time as cyclic, but instead it is like a string or straight line which is bent in a spiral shape, where at one end Time starts, and on another it ends. That brings me to a question that why haven't there been any books on Time? What might the reason for that? Maybe the Gods didn't want us to know about Time. Or maybe we are not yet ready to witness and digest the truth of Time in its true form.

For over the Time, people never bothered about it. The never really fantasized or question its existence. Years, decades, centuries, and Millennium pass by until a person, some fellow comes up with a theory on Time in its purest form with a good intention. But no matter what, there will always be people who will try to take the disadvantage of it. They will, surely because that is what is supposed to happen, because that is the destiny, and it has to be fulfilled. Therefore, someone in the upcoming years will try to break the rules of time. Which will lead to catastrophe not only for our Timeline but even will be a threat to the multiverse. Due to this a reset button will be pressed. Which will reset the timeline and start all from the beginning.

In Hindu mythology, we divide time into four yugas, or ages i.e., Satya-yuga, Tretā-yuga, Dvāpara-yuga and Kali-yuga. Many great scholars and saints, even the gods lived in the first three Yugas. It is also said that Time is supposed to end in the Kali-yuga. It starts in the satyug and is supposed to end in the kaliyug. But now the question arises is that, if Time is supposed to end in the kaliyug. Then why is this called as the 14th creation? Or why is it keep on repeating? Why is it in this cyclic form? If it was supposed to end, then there shouldn't happen any other creation. According to me, when the rules of time are broken and the proper flow of time is disturbed, we don't know who….. but someone, will press the reset button. And off goes the Timeline and reset back to the Satyug where it again starts from the beginning. All over again.

CONCLUSION

This is not the only Timeline where I have written this book, but this is the only Timeline where I have written and described it in the best version possible. All the previous concepts that have been explained, have already existed in stories and myths in varieties of different religion and cults, yet somehow are still being neglected. I believe that the key to the truth of the universe also lies somewhere in those stories, and it is just a matter of time that we might uncover the answers to the questions asked about the universe.

This Timeline has been a race against Time, fate, and destiny. Where, knowing Time is good. Understanding it, is difficult. But knowing the future is something that I personally might not call as a gift, it's a Curse of knowledge. Anything that exists in this world has already been thought in India, and what does not exist, has never been thought in India. Though there are many thoughts, works and practices that are forbidden and are beyond one's comprehension. Yet there lies a great amount of forbidden knowledge of which, neither is supposed to be said nor to be heard.

The only intension of me writing this book was to clear the doubts associated with Kāla / Time, and to showcase Kāla in its purest form as possible. Also, to explain its terrifying form in a very respectful manner. Atheists are not the only ones who don't believe in God, many do, or tend to do when Gods are not in favor. Any person who doesn't believe in God, is not trustworthy. Though any who don't believe in God or aren't scared of death, shall fear Kāla / Time.

At the end, though many might call it a fiction, fantasy, mythological or a spiritual book, I just hope this book sparks some curiosity among the readers and that their doubts have been cleared. Which, in return would consolidate me and usher a relief that this work has reached the expectations of my Guru Śiva and the quality it should have reached. Unlike Leonardo Da Vinci's last words, "I have offended God and mankind because my work did not reach the quality it should have."

A judgement or decision reached by reasoning is called conclusion, whereas here we don't need any logical reasoning or conclusion to understand the true nature of Kāla / Time. The Kāla Siddhānta unconditionally describes the true nature of time, what it is made up of and its structure. It also clears the misconception of timelines, time travelling and Multiversal structure, by standardizing all time references to a single unit called Kāla Gati and Kālanubhava. To conclude this, I recall a shloka from the Bhagavad Gita 11.32.

The supreme personality of Godhead, Lord Śri Kṛṣṇa says: "Time I am, the great destroyer of worlds, and I have come here to destroy all people. With the exception of you [the Pāṇḍavas], all the soldiers on both sides will be slain". Here Lord Śri Kṛṣṇa on the battlefield commands Arjuna to do his duty unconditionally, as he was not in favor of the fight, and he thought it was better not to fight. Where Lord Śrī Kṛṣṇa explains that even if he does not fight, everyone on the battlefield will be dead, as time consumes everything and that is the truth and the law of nature.

Looking back at my work, this Kāla Siddhānta, I sometime feel responsible for this timeline. I feel responsible for all that has happened, and all that is yet to happen. This book is supposed to be a guide, a rule book to follow and maintain the proper flow of time. But, no matter what, there will always be people to take the disadvantage of it.

MAY SIVA FORGIVE ME.

शिवः क्षमतु।।

GLOSSARY

Kāla: It is a Sanskrit term for time.

Siddhānta: It is a Sanskrit term denoting established tenet or principle or conclusion.

Śiva: He is the supreme being and one of the holy trinity in Hinduism.

Vivarana: It is a Sanskrit term for explanation or description.

Sūtra: It is a Sanskrit term for a string.

Trikālagyana: It is a Sanskrit term which means knowledge of all three states of time, i.e., past, present, and future.

Bhūta: It is a Sanskrit term for past.

Vartamāna: It is a Sanskrit term for present.

Bhaviśya: It is a Sanskrit term for future.

Sthira: It is a Sanskrit term for undisturbed or constant.

Asthira: It is a Sanskrit term for disturbed.

Niṣiddha: It is a Sanskrit term for forbidden.

Constant: Occurring continuously over a period of time

Manifold: A manifold is a topological space that is closely patterned on Euclidean space locally but may have significantly different global features. It is a generalization and abstraction of the idea of a curved surface in mathematics.

Mass: The quantity of matter in a body; its inertia, or resistance to acceleration.

General relativity: Einstein's theory based on the idea that the laws of science should be the same for all observers, no matter how they are moving. It explains the force of gravity in terms of the curvature of a four-dimensional space-time.

Special relativity: Einstein's theory based on the idea that the laws of science should be the same for all observers, no matter how they are moving, in the absence of gravitational phenomena.

Gati: It is a Sanskrit term for speed or velocity.

Kālanubhava: It is a Sanskrit term for "time experience".

Precept: A general rule intended to regulate behaviour or thought.

Thought Experiment: A thought experiment is a hypothetical situation in which a hypothesis, theory, or principle is laid out for the purpose of thinking through its consequences.

Event: A point in space-time, specified by its time and place.

Scenario: A postulated sequence or development of events.

Atom: The basic unit of ordinary matter, made up of a tiny nucleus (consisting of protons and neutrons) surrounded by orbiting electrons.

Big bang: The singularity at the beginning of the universe.

Black hole: A region of space-time from which nothing, not even light, can escape, because gravity is so strong.

Singularity: A point in space-time at which the space-time curvature becomes infinite.

Event horizon: The boundary of a black hole.

Coordinates: Numbers that specify the position of a point in space and time.

Proportional: 'X is proportional to Y' means that when Y is multiplied by any number, so is X. 'X is inversely proportional to Y' means that when Y is multiplied by any number, X is divided by that number.

Variance: Here it means a quantity or a value being different, divergent, inconsistent, or varied.

Vyāpi: It is a Sanskrit term for variance.

Bindu: It is a Sanskrit term for a point or a dot.

Gradient: change in the value of a quantity.

Speed of light: 3.00×10^8 meters/second.

Light year (light-second): The distance travelled by light in one second year.

Schwarzschild's radius: the radius below which the gravitational attraction between the particles of a body must cause it to undergo irreversible gravitational collapse.

Gravity: the force by which a planet or other body draws objects toward its center.

Universe: The universe is all of space and time and their contents, including planets, stars, galaxies, and all other forms of matter and energy.

Dimension: a measurable extent of a particular kind, such as length, breadth, depth, or height.

Dark matter: Matter in galaxies, clusters, and possibly between clusters, that cannot be observed directly but can be detected by its gravitational effect. As much as 90 percent of the mass of the universe may be in the form of dark matter.

Rekha: It is a Sanskrit term for line.

Superposition: it is the ability of a quantum system to be in multiple states at the same time until it is measured.

Prayana: It is a Sanskrit term for travelling or distance covered.

Ālekha: It is a Sanskrit term for graph.

Sīmā: It is a Sanskrit term for boundary.

Mūlādhāra: It is a Sanskrit term for root of existence.

Kāla Rekha: It is a Sanskrit term for timeline.

MūlāKāla Rekha: It is a Sanskrit term for main timeline or the primordial timeline.

Trajectory: A path, progression, or line of development resembling a physical trajectory. An upward career trajectory.

Cartesian: The cartesian form of a plane can be represented as '$ax + by + cz = d$' where a, b, and c are direction cosines that are normal to the plane and d is the distance from the origin to the plane.

Khaṇḍa: It is a Sanskrit term for parts or frames.

Saṅgraha: It is a Sanskrit term for collection.

Saṃkalana: It is a Sanskrit term for addition.

Vyavakalana: It is a Sanskrit term for division.

Prabhāvita: It is a Sanskrit term for influence or inspiration.

Samāpta: It is a Sanskrit term for ending.

Samāna: It is a Sanskrit term for same.

Asamāna: It is a Sanskrit term for different.

Multiverse: it is a hypothetical collection of potentially diverse observable universes.

MahaKāla: It is a Sanskrit term for multiverse.

Kālāntara: It is a Sanskrit term which here it means different and inter* Kāla.

MahaKālāntara: It is a Sanskrit term which here it means different and inter* MahaKāla.

Anunādaḥ: It is a Sanskrit term for resonance.

Resonance: relatively large selective response of an object or a system that vibrates in step or phase, with an externally applied oscillatory force

Frequency: For a wave, the number of complete cycles per second.

Natural frequency: It is the frequency at which a system tends to oscillate in the absence of any driving force.

Saṁkramaṇam: It is a Sanskrit term for transition.

Paradox: a statement that is seemingly contradictory or opposed to common sense and yet is perhaps true in physical descriptions of the universe.

Transition: the process or a period of changing from one state or condition to another.

Doṣa: It is a Sanskrit term for curse.

Śāstra: It is a Sanskrit term for rules.

Myths: a traditional story, especially one concerning the early history of a people or explaining a natural or social phenomenon, and typically involving supernatural beings or events.

Bhagavad Gītā: the Hindu holy text.

About the Author

Karan Londe

"Karan Londe is a passionate engineering student with a keen interest in the field of astronomy. Londe grew up and lives in Belgaum, Karnataka, India. Currently pursuing a degree in Electronics and Communication at KLE Dr. MS Sheshgiri, Belgaum. Karan has consistently demonstrated a strong aptitude for scientific research and a deep fascination with the mysteries of the cosmos.

Throughout his academic journey, Karan has actively engaged with the field of astronomy, exploring various astronomical concepts and phenomena.

This book reflects his ability to integrate theoretical knowledge with practical future applications, shedding light on intricate astronomical phenomena and offering novel perspectives.

www.ingramcontent.com/pod-product-compliance
Lightning Source LLC
LaVergne TN
LVHW041848070526
838199LV00045BA/1499